THE *DAYES* OF WYOMING

Patricia Probert Gott

*To Sally
Happy Trails
[signature: Patricia Probert Gott]*

Cover design by Patricia Probert Gott
Front Cover photo © iStockphoto.com/Gary Alvis
Layout and effects by Laura Wiley Ashton
www.gitflorida.com

Copyright © 2010 by Patricia Probert Gott.
All rights reserved.
No part of this book may be reproduced or transmitted in any form or by any electronic or mechanical means, including photocopying, recording, scanning, or by any information storage and retrieval system, without written permission from the author.

You may contact her at www.prgottbooks.net

This book is a work of fiction.

First Printing

ISBN: 978-1-4515-8522-3

Printed in the United States of America

ALSO BY PATRICIA PROBERT GOTT

Cowgirl Days

So You Wanna be a Cowgirl

Metamorphosis: My Journey of Growth and Change

Travel Novellas

Ancient Egypt and the Nile

Volunteer to Empower

Children's Stories

Horse Tails by Shasta

Horse Tails by Mookie the Mustang

Contents

THE UNLIKELY RESCUE 1

COWGIRL-UP 25

WILD HORSES .57

WINNER TAKES ALL 75

A FAMILY for WASHAKIE RANCH 93

TRIALS and TRIBULATIONS 127

THE RACE 147

EPILOGUE 169

Author's Comments 173

Northwest Wyoming

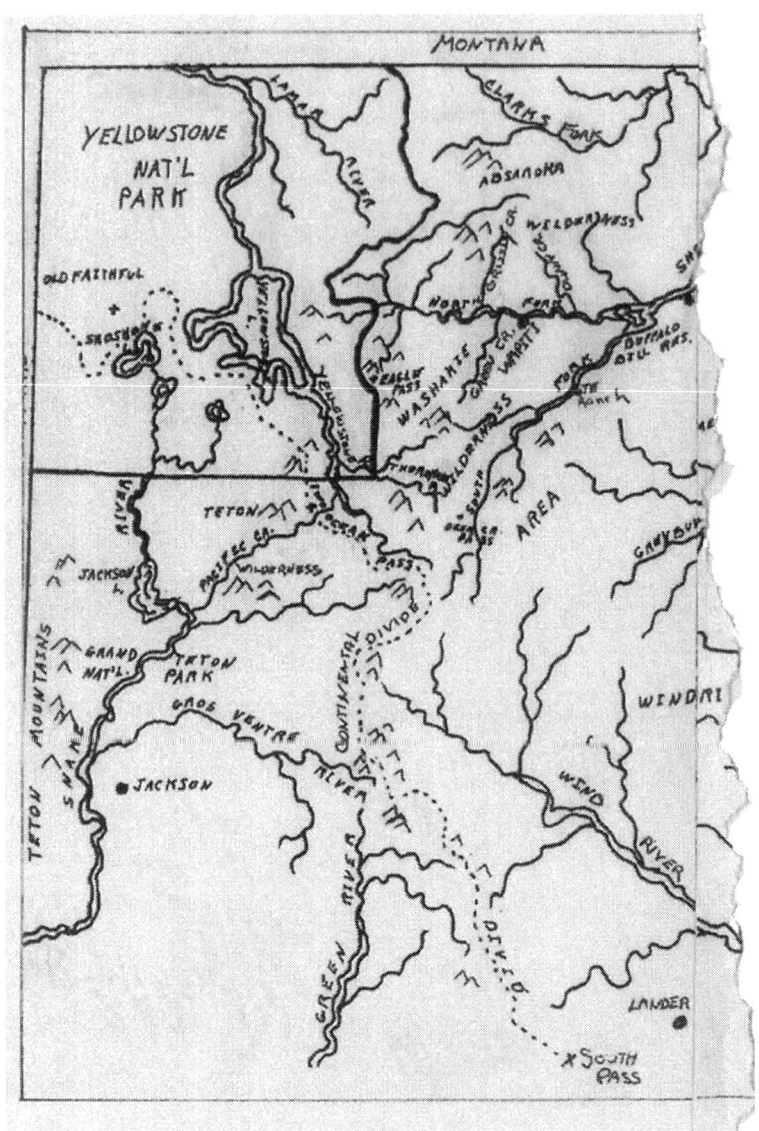

Northcentral Wyoming

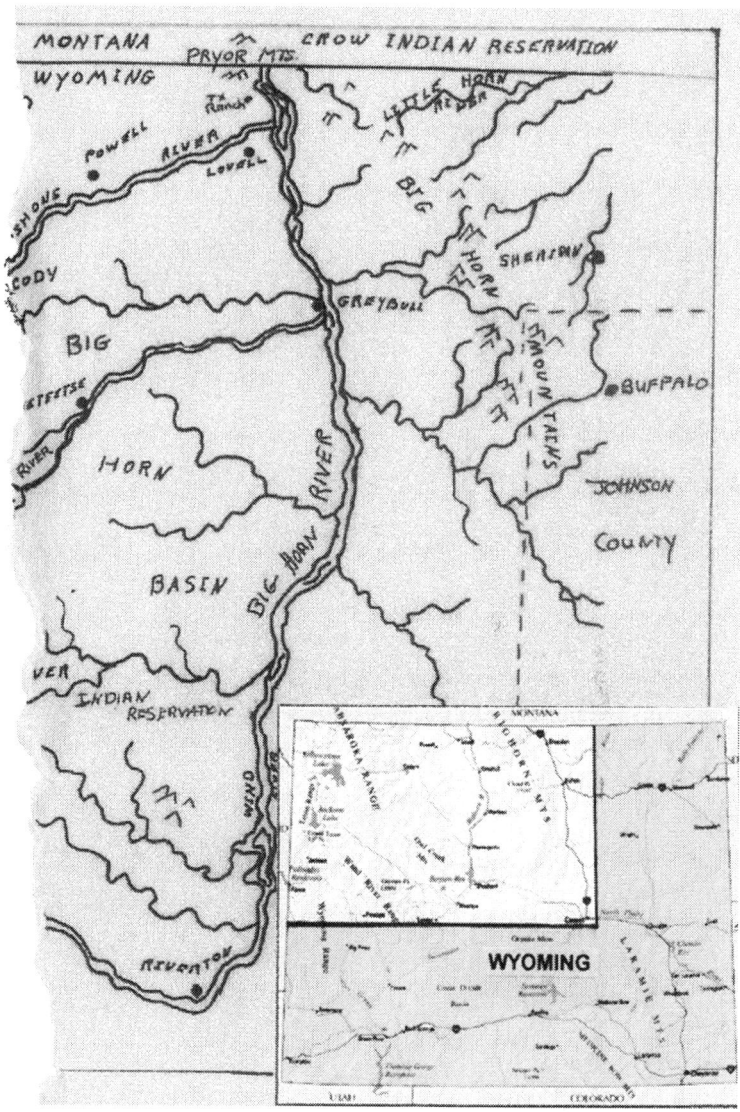

THE UNLIKELY RESCUE

History records the Johnson County War in northeast Wyoming as having taken place in 1892. But for Bertha Berry, the conflict began in 1888 the day her parents were killed.

Bertha's mother, Annie, and grandparents, Charles and Miriam Cartland, farmers from New England, traveled west on the Oregon Trail, as had thousand of others following the end of the Civil War. After losing their horses and most of their supplies in a Lakota attack, Annie and her family escaped with their lives and what belongings they could carry, and eventually wandered into Fort Fetterman. There, they settled in the nearby town of Orpha, content to live among civilization again.

Bertha's father, Henry Berry, whose family came from North Dakota, was stationed at

Fort Fetterman when the war ended. After his release from the army, he stayed in the area catching jobs at various ranches, cattle pens, and stockyards between Fort Laramie and Fort Fetterman. In 1871, Henry and Annie met and soon married. He decided to try his hand at ranching in northeastern Wyoming where his older brother, Sam, had homesteaded with his wife, Ginny. Following the Bozeman Trail from Fort Fetterman, the newlyweds claimed 160 acres of public land ten miles south of Buffalo, in Johnson County.

A few years and one girl-child later, Mr. and Mrs. Berry found their acreage too small to graze cattle profitably. They tried farming. However, two summers in a row of extreme heat and drought followed by severe cold and winter blizzards left them desperate.

So in the mid- to late 1880s, as other small ranchers and homesteaders had taken to doing, Henry rounded up unbranded calves every spring before the big ranch roundups, put his own brand on them, and created a herd out of thin air. It was considered legal to brand year-old mavericks. However, branding another rancher's calves was rustling—illegal—plain and simple.

* * *

Born a natural horsewoman, Bertha preferred being in the saddle working cattle with her stern and dour-faced father to helping her mother, whose former sunny disposition and beauty were fading fast. When a young horse needed training, her father would rope, hobble and buck it until it submitted or died, until Bertha resurrected a fallen horse one day by gentle care and communication. From then on, when she was not attending school, it became Bertha's job to train young, stubborn, or mean horses. Her mother insisted she go to school through the 8th grade, where she excelled in reading and arithmetic. However, her greatest love would always be horses. Even helping her father round up and brand calves, which her mother said was illegal and dangerous, didn't bother her because she loved to be on the open range, on horseback all day, riding her red-chestnut gelding, Flame. Being of young teenage years and mindset, she did not comprehend *rustling* or *danger*.

Many times, large cattle ranchers (also called barons) hauled cattle rustlers (thieves) into court, but it was almost impossible to get a local jury to convict anyone. Finally, the barons of Johnson County decided to take matters into their own hands. With emotions running high, agents (hired guns) of the larger ranches began burning smaller farms and killing alleged rustlers.

Bertha and her father were riding through a narrow draw heading back to their ranch pushing a dozen newly branded calves ahead of them when the first shots rang out. Henry yelled, "Get down, Bertha. Hide behind those rocks yonder."

She leaped off Flame leaving him to fend for himself as she dove for cover behind the boulders. Looking behind her, she could see her father pulling himself along trying to reach the rocks also. He'd been shot in the leg. "Pop," she screamed, as she ran to him.

"No. Go back," he shouted. She paid no attention and began dragging him as best she could for a small-built girl.

More rounds of gunshots, hitting Henry twice in the back.

"What do you want?" she called out, naively thinking the gunmen were robbers. "We don't have money. Take the horses. Please don't shoot any more," she sobbed, holding her father's head in her lap as he lay still, blood seeping from his mouth, eyes still open.

"Ohmygosh. That one's a girl," one of the gunmen said in shock.

"Let her be; she'll do us no more harm." The

leader signaled the rest to mount up. "Let's ride," he said, and the three men were gone, leaving Bertha grieving for her dead father.

What to do now, she wondered. *I can't leave him here in the open—I must get him back to the ranch and to Mom. She'll know what to do.*

Bertha whistled to her gelding. When he came, she signaled him to lie down as she had taught him. Struggling, she hoisted her father onto Flame's back and asked him to stand. Tying her father over the saddle, she mounted their other horse and led Flame.

The horror of the day unfolded as she rode toward the safety of home and her mother; tears spilled from her red-rimmed eyes. However, more tragedy was forthcoming as she crested the bluff above their farm and peered down at the burnt timbers, smoke and ashes that were all that remained of their cabin.

She spurred her horse to a gallop until she reached the barn, calling, "Mom. Mom. Where are you? Are you alright?"

No answer. . . silence, except for the snap and crackle of still-smoldering logs.

Bertha found her mother's charred remains. Neighbors helped bury her parents on the bluff overlooking their 160 acres. The killers remained anonymous.

In 1889, the infamous double lynching of innocents Ella Watson and storekeeper Jim Averell enraged local residents to the point of forming their own Northern Wyoming Farmers and Stock Grower's Association, with Nate Champion as their foreman.

****

Johnson County GAZETTE
July, 1889

Homesteader Ella Watson and storekeeper Jim Averell accused of cattle rustling... and hanged.

****

A number of additional dubious lynchings of alleged rustlers took place in 1891.

In 1892, Frank M. Canton, former sheriff of Johnson County, was hired by the barons to lead a band of Texas killers, and Nate Champion was murdered at his KC Ranch—thus began Wyoming's Civil War, which became known as the Johnson County War.

After a shootout at the TA Ranch, which

resulted in several men being killed, the governor of Wyoming described the conflict as an insurrection against the government and wired President Benjamin Harrison requesting he call out Fort McKinney's Sixth Cavalry near Buffalo for "protection from invasion and domestic violence." They were to stop the violence, restore order and arrest the barons' hired killer expedition.

Court proceedings dragged on, material witnesses disappeared, and, ultimately, the high cost of the trial led the court to dismiss the entire case. Though the Johnson County Cattle War was declared over in a matter of a few weeks, scattered violence continued for more than a decade as rustlers continued to be hanged. The long-term legacy was that Johnson County was slower to develop economically than some other parts of the state due to the view that the county was a volatile place to live.

* * *

By the end of the Cattle War, Bertha was long gone, having moved north to Sheridan County with her father's brother, Sam and his wife, Ginny.

After the fire, Sam and his wife had showed up

laying claim to the 160 acres. Bertha had already agreed to sell the land to adjacent neighbors, and Sam had no rightful claim to the land anyway. He then offered to look after her, for a fee, until she reached adulthood or married.

Sam's family had lived nearby, and he often took part in the cattle thievery, so he was anxious to move out of the county before gunmen came for him too. He told Bertha they planned to travel, at once, to a small farm Ginny's family had left her near Sheridan, Wyoming. With no other foreseeable options (plus she was anxious to leave the feuding area behind), Bertha traveled north with them where they settled on Wolf Creek. She worked, paying her own way by training young and cantankerous horses. She had decided she would save the money from the sale of the ranch to buy a place of her own someday, so she deposited half in the Sheridan Trust Bank and hid the other half with her saddles and gear in the barn's tack room.

Sam drank too much liquor and frequented saloons every day. He was a mean drunk prone to a nasty temper. Their two boys left home as soon as they could find jobs. Bertha stayed clear of him most of the time, content to stay in her space in the barn with the animals. When Sam was not drunk or hung over, he would ride around the county selling Bertha's talents as a horse trainer. He would find horses for her to train and bring them back to the ranch . . . for a 50% commission. The fee was steep, but she didn't mind as she didn't know anyone in this part of the state and loved her work regardless of the money.

"Hey, Bertha, looky this one I got fer you to train. Ain't he somethin'?" Sam said when he came home one morning reeking of liquor after being out all night. He had undoubtedly brought her another biting, kicking, sour youngster who had been bucked, half broke, then left to pasture.

Bertha observed a big four-year-old bay gelding with beautiful lines, an aggressive attitude, and full of himself. He had rope scars on his neck from pulling back and on his legs from being hobbled too closely with thin rawhide. With his ears pinned back and teeth bared, she took his lead rope and led him to a small pen that she used for training, also containing fresh hay and water. She had to elbow him three times when he kept nipping at her on the way to the pen. "You'll soon stop that, young man," she said to him, using a low voice so Sam wouldn't hear her and criticize her, again, for being so soft. He never watched her train, which set well with her as she didn't like his manner around horses or his negative comments. She liked being alone, especially while training.

She trained horses with a combination of dominance, respect, and communication using body language that horses naturally understood from their heritage. She crooned to them and talked softly but firmly when she first started gentling them. Later she would add single words in a given tone to tell the horse what she wanted from him. She found that most problem horses had just not grasped what the owner wanted, got frustrated, then fought in self-defense.

She watched the bay drink his fill, explore his pen, then settle down to chew on the hay. She liked the way he moved. She whistled, his ears pricked up and he stopped chewing. She began whistling a tune, and he watched her intently as he went back to eating, keeping one eye on her. "Good boy," she said. "We'll start training tomorrow morning and see how you do."

Using her three training tools: dominance, respect and body language—sometimes separately, sometimes together—Bertha began moving the bay around the pen. She had removed his halter and any obstructions from the pen. She carried a coiled rope, which she used to help keep the bay moving first in one direction, then the other, at a trot and then at a lope. As he became slightly winded, he began looking at her and slowing down—he wanted to stop and seemed to be asking permission.

She said a firm "Whoa," letting him to come to a halt; he faced her as if to say, Now what? She allowed him his space for a minute, then walked up to him a step at a time and patted his forehead saying "Good boy." He flinched, shifted his feet, and she sent him moving around the pen again.

The next time he stopped, faced her and relaxed, she moved halfway toward him; then she made a kissing sound and backed up. He followed. She patted his forehead, praised him and began caressing his neck and withers—no biting so far. While talking in a soft voice, she continued to run her hand down his chest, barrel, flanks and hindquarters—so far, so good. When she touched his hock, he lifted his hind leg as if to kick, so she moved him a few more times around the pen.

The bay soon got the message that *she* controlled what he did, and when. If he submitted, he received praise and pats; if he resisted, she made him move at whatever speed she decided. She put his halter back on with ease, and he followed her anywhere at any speed without a lead rope. She left him untied and sacked him out with saddle blankets, cow bells, and rain slickers. . . anything she could find to teach him to trust that, no matter what, she wasn't going to let him be hurt. She led him to the side where she could step on a rail and leaned her weight over his body. If he moved, she made him run around the pen. She finally slipped onto him bareback, sat for a minute, not wanting to push her luck too far, and then slid off. She scratched his neck, heaped praises on him, and stopped for the day.

The next morning after feeding the animals and eating her own breakfast of cold biscuits and warm milk, she went to the pen to begin working with the bay. He even seemed happy to see her, or he was just lonely for company. She began talking to him as she first put a saddle pad on his back, then strapped on a saddle; "I think I'll call you Rocky. Seems to suit you as you're solid as a rock. How do you like that name, fella?"

She moved him around the pen letting the stirrups dangle and bang against his flanks. Today she added a single word to each body language gesture: *walk, trot, lope, whoa, over* and *back*. These words would reinforce her signals once she was on his back. After practicing each movement and word several times, she slipped a bosal headstall on him, took both reins in one hand, put her left boot in the stirrup, lifted her weight and stood in the stirrup for a couple of seconds. Then she stepped back onto the ground, patted his neck and praised him, "Good boy, Rocky." The next time, she lifted her weight off the ground and eased her right leg over the saddle, sat for a minute, patted him, and gently dismounted. This she repeated several times, sitting longer each time. Then, while astride, she practiced pulling his head to one side then the other to accustom and soften his head to her hand cues.

His final test for the morning came when she asked him to move while she was on his back. "Walk," she said as she moved his head a little to the side and squeezed with her legs. He humped his back but did not buck. When he moved his feet any direction, he received pats and praises, moving further each time as he learned that that was what she wanted and that he was not going to be hurt. Periodically, she tugged slightly on both reins saying, "Whoa." For the morning, that was his favorite word.

The next day, lessons progressed more quickly, although she always repeated each step before advancing to a new command. Within the next few days, he learned to move out at a walk and a trot and to back up on cue. She would have liked to have someone ride with her the first time she took Rocky out of the pen, but she preferred going alone to having Sam go with her, and Ginny didn't ride.

She rode him every day for the next couple of weeks, taking him further from the farm each time, exposing him to riding ridges, ravines, and through creeks. He grew more confident each day.

Bertha was just preparing to mount Rocky for a quiet ride one morning when Sam appeared at the corral, still near drunk and stinking from carousing in town for the past three days.

"How's that mean cayuse doin'? Seen you ridin' him the other day an' think it's 'bout time I checked to see how good a job you done, bein' all soft and easy on him," he said as he staggered toward her. "Now give me those reins like a good girl and hold him still whist I get my foot in the stirrup."

Rocky snorted and moved around nervously.

"No, he's not ready for anyone else to ride him yet," she said, determined not to let Sam near Rocky, much less ride him. "I don't want you messing up my training for the owner."

"*I* own him, Miss Smarty Britches. He's **mine**. I won 'im at poker and I'll do whatever I wanna," he slurred. He grabbed the reins from Bertha, and Rocky pulled back in fright.

"Come here you mangy cayuse and I'll give you somethin' so's you'll know who's boss," he snarled. He drew back and hit Rocky in the head with his fist as Bertha yelled, "Nooooo," and plowed into Sam's mid-section knocking him to the ground. Rocky screamed, reared and came down on Sam's right arm and shoulder. Sam passed out.

Ginny burst from the cabin. "Bertha, what's happening? What's all the fuss out here?"

"Sam's drunk and hit the horse in the head, so I knocked him down and the horse stepped on him," she explained, minimizing Rocky's part.

"I need to get out of here. When Sam comes to, he'll be madder than a grizzly woke up in dead winter. I'm afraid he'll hurt the horse, or me."

"I think you're right, dear, but where will you go?"

"I don't know, but I can't stay here any longer. I'll help you haul Sam inside, then I'm going to think on it while I gather my things."

What she found as she got her tack together and saddled Flame was that most of her money was missing from her saddlebags where she'd hidden them in the tack room. *That son-of-a-gun stole my money,* she said to herself. *That's what he's been using to buy all his liquor. I bet he bought Rocky with that money too. Guess I'll just take Rocky with me seeing as he was paid for with my money.*

She stormed into the cabin telling Ginny that Sam stole her money and she was packing what she needed; she was owed. She took a pot, skillet, cup, utensils, flour, sugar, coffee, matches, ammunition, and one of Sam's rifles from the cabin. She took a packsaddle from the tack room and fit it to Rocky; she'd lead him and ride Flame. She packed her bedroll, slicker, what clothes she owned, along with feed, hobbles and ropes for the horses; then covered it all with a tarp.

As she rode past the cabin, she felt sorry for Ginny having to put up with Sam's eventual wrath, but she had her own life, and her horses, to consider. She focused on finding her way to the western side of the Bighorn Mountains. . . far away from Sam Berry, and Johnson County.

It took Bertha five days to cross the Bighorns into open rangeland with no fences, ranches, or homesteads in sight. Lucky for her it was late spring, the snow lay in small patches and game still plentiful in the mountains. The horses were doing well maintaining their weight on spring grasses. She camped beside Big Horn Lake for a week before moving on.

She figured she needed to stay away from towns for a while, as she didn't know if Sam would lie to the Sheridan sheriff and have him send wires throughout the states claiming she was a thief. She could not prove he had stolen her money. She'd heard that many mustangs ran wild around the Pryor Mountains in Montana, so maybe she'd go north and camp among them; she was sure they would accept her presence within a short while. Eventually, she mused, she could catch jobs at ranches as an itinerant wrangler training their horses without bucking them to death or breaking their spirit.

Her daydreaming ended when she noticed the small town of Lovell coming into view. Skirting the town with care, she circled north toward the mountains. A couple days later, looking down on a long valley, she spotted a Crow hunting party riding east. Her heart froze. She promptly rode west well into the evening. Not daring to shoot game for fear of Indians hearing her rifle report, she set a snare to see if she could catch a jackrabbit or some other small game for supper.

She unloaded her camp gear, hobbled her horses for the evening, and then wandered a few hundred yards until she found a stand of juniper where she set a rope snare. She had begun to doze off behind some sage bushes when approaching hoofbeats startled her wide awake. Not quite in a state of panic, yet, she sneaked back to camp and grabbed her rifle ready to shoot the first Indian she saw. Silence: no hoof beats, no moving brush, no Indians.

Click. She heard the sound of a gun being cocked right behind her. "Don't move," said a man's voice. "Drop your gun an' turn 'round, slow-like.

"Well, ma'am," the man said, grinning when he saw she was a pretty young woman, "jus' who ya plannin' on shootin'?"

"Indians," she snapped, sizing him up to be neither Indian nor cowboy by his fur tunic, leggings, and mules.

"Well, I ain't Injun, so how's 'bout calling a truce," he said lowering his gun.

"What are you, or who are you?" she said, getting more perturbed at her situation by the minute. "I'm Bertha. This is *my* camp and I intend to defend it."

"I can see that," he said, not unkindly. "Name's Charlie Daye, mountain man from over near Yellowstone. Don't mean ya no harm; I'm jus' sensitive to having someone draw a bead on me whist I'm mindin' my own business, takin' some hides to Cody."

Charlie Daye owned some land, a small cabin, and shelter for his mules in an area called Wapiti, between Cody and Yellowstone National Park, on the North Fork of the Stinking Water River, later known as the Shoshone. He was around 30 years old, tall, slim, and would be considered nice-looking if he cleaned up. He was the son of a Shawnee woman named White Fox and Nathan Daye, who was a third-generation mountain man, having hunted and trapped with the likes of Jeremiah Johnson and Jim Bridger. Charlie was kind and gentle, didn't talk much, loved the mountains and his mules—and he was unmarried.

"Well, why don't you tie or hobble your mules and come sit. I'll make us some coffee, if I have any left; I'm sorta running a little short on supplies. I was setting a snare for some supper, if we haven't scared all the game away. . . why don't you join me?" She was babbling out of nervousness. She began busying herself making a fire, boiling water for coffee, and checking her snare, trying to collect her thoughts enough to carry on an understandable conversation.

They ate in easy silence while enjoying the roasted hare. Bertha used the last of her flour to make biscuits, and her coffee supply was down to just enough for breakfast. Sensing her tension as she emptied her supply sacks, and without prying into why she was alone in these mountains, Charlie offered, "Why don't ya accompany me into Cody whilst I do some tradin'? It's 'nother couple days' ride or so, and you're welcome to share my food 'til ya get restocked in town; that is, if ya keep your rifle sheathed and not go pointin' it at me again." He smiled.

Bertha felt she could trust him. . . but maybe not enough to tell him her whole story. She replied, "I don't need charity, but I'd appreciate riding with you, for a ways at least, until we get past possible Indians on the prowl."

She did have a dilemma, however, because even though she needed more supplies, she wasn't sure it was safe to show up in town. She would have to wait and see. Meanwhile, she would just ride along and enjoy the safety of traveling with her newfound acquaintance.

It took two days to reach Cody. Charlie killed a small antelope for supper one evening, Bertha cooked biscuits and beans from his food supply. She was beginning to feel real comfortable around him as he never plied her with questions, although he answered hers with readiness. The night before reaching Cody, she felt she needed to confide her dilemma and explain her reluctance to ride into town with him. Once she began, she didn't stop talking until she'd spilled her entire story from rustling and her parents being killed in Johnson County to her Uncle Sam, horse training, running away, and suspected thievery.

"There," she said, on the verge of tears, "that's my story and why I'm alone. You probably don't want me riding with you anymore, and I don't blame you, so thanks for your hospitality and I'll be gone tomorrow morning so's not to cause you any trouble." She was babbling again.

Charlie sat in silence for a few minutes smoking his pipe. "Well," he mused, "people might not be so anxious to suspect ya if you were my new bride. I'm purty well thought of, so they might just think well of ya too. Don't need to do the real thing if'n ya don't want, but pretendin' sometimes comes back to kick ya in the britches."

Bertha was stunned. . . speechless.

She walked off to locate Rocky and Flame, her mind spinning like a coyote chasing his tail. She could find solace in talking to them.

True, Charlie was an honorable man; he'd not tried anything untoward while she'd been camping with him; he seemed hardworking and honest, and had treated her with kindness and respect. He wasn't a drinking man, as he carried no alcohol with him, and his temper was mellow, not feisty. Besides, she pondered, being married to him might help her out of her present predicament with the law; she could see just one possible downside.

She tramped back to the campfire and stated emphatically, "I ain't gonna be no stay-at-home kitchen cook, cabin cleaner or baby raiser. I can be a good partner to you, but I don't wanna lose who I am—which is a horse trainer. Would that be agreeable to you?"

"Yes, dear, that would be right fine by me," Charlie answered, suppressing a smile.

* * *

A Lutheran preacher in Cody married Bertha and Charlie the next day. They developed an easy affection for one another and soon became an unbeatable team, whether outfitting guests into the mountains, scouting for the government, or training horses... their reputation impeccable.

COWGIRL-UP

Bertha Daye sat at the bar of the Irma Hotel in Cody, Wyoming finishing a shot of whiskey. She and her husband, Charlie, had just spent three months down on the South Fork of the Shoshone working for the government scouting and counting what remained of small bison herds. She had been too long in the saddle. Fixed up, she was fair-looking and cut a fine figure for a woman doing man's work, horse training and wrangling. Her blond hair, usually long and wavy, was now ingrained with sweat and dirt, making it as stiff as a horse's tail. She threatened to hack it off short whenever it fell in her face while fixing chow or shoeing her horse. But her husband liked it long, so she acquiesced to his wishes—on this matter.

She always told him he was the boss. "It's easier that way," she would say, "then we don't have to waste time arguing. He knows men, mountains and mules; I take care of the rest and he doesn't complain." Bertha was best known for her independence, spunk and feistiness, as well as her honesty and hard work.

Charlie was a handsome tall drink of water with long gray-streaked hair and a short gray beard. His weathered wrinkles revealed he was at least 12 to 14 years older than Bertha. He downed his second shot and said, "Hey, Dave, let's have another round. Been long time in them mountains and worked up quite a thirst. This here bar is sure somethin' special, ain't it? Smells purty too, like wood flowers in the spring."

"You old fool," Bertha said, "that's cherry wood, come clear across the ocean as a gift to Bill Cody from Queen Victoria herself. . . so I heard tell. And look at them wall-to-wall mirrors in back; hope they don't get broke in some rowdy brawl. Just finished up building her. Let's get us a room upstairs; heard they's real fancy. And we could try out one of them feather beds," she added with a wink.

"First, I need a long hot bath," she said as she climbed off the stool. "I stink worse than a mule's rear end. You got tubs up there in one of those rooms don't you Dave?"

"Yes, ma'am. I'll have Doris started carrying

some hot water for you."

"Now don't go calling me Ma'am; sounds like you want something when you do that."

"Okay, ma'am. I mean, Bertha. I'll get on it right away."

"Now Charlie, don't you be drinking too much or you won't be no good to me. I'll be expecting you in a couple of hours, cleaned up and shaved, if you want some goodies."

"Yes, ma'am," he answered with a grin.

That evening as Bertha and Charlie sat eating at the Irma, Bill Cody charged through the double doors. "Hey, Charlie, Bertha, nice to see you again."

The three had met at the town of Cody's incorporation celebration the summer of 1901. Bertha had tried to bargain Bill's white Arabian stallion from him after winning a high-stake poker game in which he ended up keeping the stallion but owing her money. He'd paid on the debt every time they'd met after that. They had become good friends though Bertha still chided him about wanting to own his stallion.

"You like the hotel now that it's finished?" he asked as he strode over to their table, shaking their hands with vigor before grabbing a chair beside Charlie.

"Named it for my daughter... ain't it something? 'Best in the West,' so they say.

"So, how long you folks around?" Bill spewed out before either had a chance to answer his first question.

"Bertha and I just rode into town this mornin' from being down on the South Fork; we passed your TE Ranch a couple days back. We may head up the North Fork in a few days.

"Say, I heard there's gonna be some big doings west of town in the canyon... somethin' about the Reclamation Service building a dam between Rattlesnake and Cedar. You have anything to do with that?"

"Yep," Bill said. "I belong to the Wyoming Board of Land Commissioners, and we've been after the federals to step in and help with our irrigation development. They're supposed to start blasting next year, creating a huge water-storage reservoir. Be a mess for a while, but eventually it will be a godsend to the valley ranches, mine included.

"By the way, been looking for someone to take four city-folk guests of mine packhorse camping for a few days, or a week. They're holed up at my lodge in Wapiti right now. They hail from Virginia, come up from Denver coupla weeks ago. Are you folks interested in making some money? You say you're headed that direction anyway."

Every since Yellowstone had become a national park, people from the East had been traveling to the West to recapture the feelings of nostalgia for bygone days. As Nathaniel P. Langdon described Yellowstone, ". . . your memory becomes filled and clogged with objects new in experience, wonderful in extent, and possessing unlimited grandeur and beauty."

No wonder "greenhorns" (or "dudes") were paying high prices to come west to experience a somewhat edited version of the pack trip life of mountain men or ranch life of cowboys.

"My eastern guests say they want excitement! Speaking of which, you two want to come to my Wild West Show tomorrow? I'll introduce you to Annie Oakley. She got hurt real bad in a railway crash a year or so ago, but she's back with the show for this one last season. What a hotshot! You'd like her."

"What time and where?" Bertha asked before Bill could begin another nonstop spiel.

"The parade begins here at the Irma around noon and ends at my showground, set up east of town, where we entertain for a few hours. Here's a couple of tickets. Let's meet here for dinner tomorrow evening and talk some more. Give you a chance to decide whether you want to guide this group of mine."

And with that, he was gone like a tornado cutting across a prairie.

"Whew, he's a man in a hurry. . . makes me dizzy just listening to him; he talks so fast."

"So what do ya think, dear? Want to take Bill's guests into the mountains?"

"Sure," Bertha said. "The money would be welcome. Give me and the animals a couple days to rest up and we'll be set to go."

On his "water-smooth silver stallion," Bill led his "Wild West and Congress of Rough Riders of the World Parade on Horseback." Following him were a variety of participants including the U.S. military, American Indians and performers from all over the world, all in their best dress. There were Gauchos from South America, Turks, Arabs, Mongols, and Cossacks, each displaying their distinctive horse breeds and colorful costumes.

The show was intense—just like Bill—speed and noise abounded. Authentic western personalities appeared, like Sitting Bull with a band of 20 Sioux warriors. Buffalo Bill and his troupe re-enacted the riding of the Pony Express, Indian attacks on wagon trains and stagecoach robberies. Annie Oakley and her husband, Frank Butler, put on shooting exhibitions along with Gabriel Dumont.

"Did you see that, Charlie? Oakley just put five bullet holes from her .22 in a playing card before it touched the ground. Amazing!"

"Yep. I wouldn't have believed it if I hadn't seen it with my own eyes. Do ya want to meet her later? Bill said he'd introduce us."

"Nah. I'd rather think of her as someone mystical, not a real person; she's too perfect. Let's go back to town and start preparing for another trip."

The Wild West Show ended with a melodramatic re-enactment of Custer's Last Stand; Cody himself portrayed General Custer.

After another luxurious respite in the hot-water tub, Bertha sauntered downstairs in her new outfit: a cream-colored, front-ruffled, long-sleeved blouse and a light-brown suede, split skirt she had purchased at the Cody General that afternoon. Looking around the dining area, she spotted Charlie and Bill at the bar.

"Wow, don't you look like a ray of sunshine all gussied up!" Bill commented as she joined them. "Charlie, you'd better keep a snug hold on her; she's a looker and. . . ouch," he said as she slugged him, half kidding, half serious, on the arm.

"Let's find a table and have some dinner before the shit gets any deeper," Bertha said leading the way.

During dinner, they discussed the show and performers and finally got around to Bill's proposed pack trip. "Bertha and I have decided to guide your guests. Ya say there are four of 'em; any idea where they'd like to travel?"

"Whereas they're already in Wapiti, why don't you take them further up the North Fork to Eagle Creek into Three-Mile-Meadow?"

"Good idea. We could continue over Eagle Pass down the Yellowstone into the Thorofare. That's a nice trek, plenty of game. . . good fishin'. We could lay over a day or two there and see how well the dudes' survivin' before we decide about the return trek."

"Three of them will do fine; the fourth I'm not too sure about," Bill said.

"We could come back through the valleys of Pass Creek into the Ishawooa, then drop them at your TE Ranch on the South Fork if they turn out to be real wimpy," Bertha added. "Or if they want excitement, we can return by way of Rampart Pass; that trek is sure to give them a thrill. Then we'd follow Elk Fork Creek back to Wapiti."

"We'll just have to play it by ear. Sounds like we'll be out eight to ten days," Charlie said. "Is that the length of trip your guests are looking for, Bill?"

"Yep. I'll send a rider up to Wapiti Inn to

tell them to be ready to travel in. . . what, four days?"

"Make it five. My horses and mules need a few more days' rest, and I need to look over and repair gear and harnesses."

"These dandies are going to need some pampering and special handling, so why don't you look up young Larry Motts and see if he'll come along to help free me up some. And I need to purchase food staples, and check the stock's hooves," Bertha added.

"I'll leave you folks to handle the logistics. My guests are prepared to pay plenty, so don't spare the expense. My show is moving on to Cheyenne for the winter the day after tomorrow, so if I don't see you before I go—have a great trip."

"Thanks for the business, Bill."

Bertha added, "And if you decide you ever want to sell that stallion of yours, you know I want first dibs at him. He's one helluva piece of horseflesh."

"Not much chance of that," he countered good-naturedly as he sped out the door.

* * *

The mules and horses were rested, feet

trimmed and shoes replaced if needed, harnesses mended, food staples like flour, sugar, salt, coffee, beans, bacon and precious eggs packed in panniers beneath buffalo skins to keep them fresh. Other panniers, containing cookware and maintenance supplies, hung on the mules' packsaddles, covered with canvas and tied down with rope. Axes, shovels and bulky items slid in between the ropes. Rifles, bedrolls, and saddlebags for miscellaneous items, hung from the riding horses' saddles.

Charlie had found Larry Motts working at the livery; he was more than willing to hire on for the trek. Larry was a good-looking man in his early twenties, honest, muscular and not afraid of hard work. He'd worked for the Dayes' on a trek to Jackson Hole the previous year.

"Move 'em out," yelled Charlie. It was his traditional way of commencing a trip and motivating his mules, tied head to tail, to move forward. First came Charlie riding his buckskin mustang leading his five pack mules, then Bertha on her smart-looking bay quarter horse, Rocky, leading two of the guests' horses, followed by Larry riding his own black-spotted Appaloosa leading the other two guests' horses. Not knowing beforehand the size or weight of the guests, Charlie had brought along part-draft horses for them to ride, and being sturdy animals, these horses could also be used to pack if necessary.

Charlie found the canyon west of Cody passable but congested with surveyors, engineers and construction equipment. *Folks from the North Fork will have to cross the Shoshone and come into Cody from the south if this canyon gets anymore crowded,* he thought to himself.

As they left the arid land surrounding Cody, following the Shoshone north, they began seeing broad pastures of cattle and horses, hand-hewn fences, fields of rich alfalfa grass, hay stacked outside barn corrals and windmills pumping stock water from the river. *A land of plenty,* Bertha mused as she rode behind her husband and his mules.

Hills on both sides of the dirt road grew steeper as the pack team continued west at a ground-covering walk. While stopping to water the stock at the river's edge, they took advantage of the cottonwoods' shade to break for a light lunch and rest the animals. "We should arrive in Wapiti Valley by late afternoon," Charlie said. They were making good time, as the road winding between the hills was still level.

They pulled into Wapiti Inn's stock corrals at feed time, unloaded their packs and stored them under canvas tarps. After feeding and watering their horses and mules, they entered the lodge hungry for some grub themselves—a vacant table caught their eye.

As they sat down, a well-endowed matron in a blue gingham dress and white apron came from the kitchen with her hand outstretched. "Howdy, I'm Cora. You must be the Daye outfitters."

"Yes, ma'am," Charlie stood and shook her hand. "This is my wife, Bertha, and extra hand, Larry Motts." Everyone exchanged "hellos."

"The Masons are all sitting right over there; I'll introduce them to you after dinner. We have plenty of beef stew and homemade bread; hope that's okay. I'll bring it out shortly," Cora said as she retreated into her kitchen.

"Charlie," Bertha whispered, "two of them's women and fancy ones at that! I wonder if they knows how tough a horse pack trip can be on even the best of men riders."

"Well, guess they'll find out purty soon, won't they. Bill said they wanted a mountain trek experience and we'll give 'em one—men and women. Wyoming is an equality state, right? Women can vote—women can horse trek."

"Oh my," was all Bertha could say.

Cora made brief introductions after dinner, "Alice and Albert Mason, Louise and John Mason, meet Bertha and Charlie Daye and Larry Motts."

It was easy to note that the two men were brothers but hard to tell them apart with their fair skin, medium build, and blond hair cut the same length, although Albert was a mite taller. The ladies were very different; dark-haired Alice appeared the picture of femininity, small and dainty while Louise was a strapping redhead.

"Pleased to meet ya," Charlie said. "I'll keep this short. We can socialize once we're at campsite. Ya need to pack light: bring one extra set of clothes, a heavy jacket, boots, gloves, hat, and rain slicker; that's about all you'll need. Meet at the corrals just after daybreak. See ya in the mornin'."

An early start was necessary so they could take an hour break to rest and eat lunch and still reach their campsite near Eagle Creek trailhead by late afternoon. The guests arrived punctually. Louise wore an appropriate split skirt; Alice wore a dress.

Bertha groaned as she left saddling her gelding to go correct the situation. "Alice, you look wonderful for a day in Cody, but not to ride horseback 25 miles a day, up mountains and down. You need to be wearin' a split skirt or pants."

"But all I have are dresses; I'll be perfectly okay in a sidesaddle."

"Ma'am, we use only stock saddles. Borrow a pair of your husband's breeches and you'll do fine." With that, Bertha whipped around and stomped back to her horse cursing under her breath... *city slickers be damned.*

The first leg of the trip continued to follow the trodden road to Yellowstone. Hills turned into evergreen- and aspen-covered mountains upon leaving Wapiti Valley. The scenery was magnificent and the riding easy. Everyone rode in relative quiet enjoying the views, the blue sky and warming sunshine. The lady guests rode with one leg draped around the horn imitating a sidesaddle pose. Bertha held her tongue, as their riding position would not matter until they hit the mountainous trails tomorrow.

Many outfitters packing into the Yellowstone area used the trailhead at Eagle Creek; therefore, corrals, hay and water were available for the animals. They set up camp on level ground next to the creek. Two guest fly tents, consisting of a canvas tarp held up by two poles and ropes tied to tree limbs, were erected on the perimeter for their comfort. Bedrolls spread atop a second tarp. The pack crew slept on their saddle blankets with a buffalo robe pulled over for warmth when necessary.

That evening, Bertha, designated social director, spoke to the women about personal comforts (or discomforts as they might be).

"There are no outhouses in the forests," she

began, "so when you feel the urge to relieve yourself around camp, you'll take the spade and a wipe to the woods with you and bury your waste—no exceptions. The rule of pack trips is that 'you leave the forests as you find them.' There are no bathtubs either, but you can fill a washbasin with hot water from the kettle we keep on the fire at all times or use cold water from the creeks we'll camp beside. Any questions?" The ladies said nothing, clearly intimidated by her candor.

"Oh, one more thing, Alice, for your own safety, you will ride astride your horse beginning tomorrow. From here on, we leave the road and ride trails across rivers, up banks, over blowdowns, across ledges, up mountains and down. Keeping your own balance and not interfering with your horse is vital, especially on an 18-inch trail along the side of a 9500-foot-high mountain cliff. We want everyone to enjoy themselves but be safe." By now, the ladies' faces were pallid.

Soon after sunrise the next morning, with Charlie leading three mules and Larry leading two, the group crossed Eagle Creek from the trailhead. The guests followed, and Bertha brought up the rear.

Eagle Creek proved too deep for the last and smaller mule (named Stump) Larry was leading. He lost his footing and would have been swept down river except that his lead rope held, allowing Larry's horse and the other mule to pull him across. Stump's pack kept him afloat. The robe covering his pack got wet, but it would be dry in a short time once they got moving up the trail. He wasn't upset and he quietly grazed his horse while waiting for the rest to cross.

That was too much excitement, too soon, for Alice. She refused to ride across. Bertha rode forward and grabbed the horse's reins, yelling, "Hang on and do not move. It's either stay in the saddle or swim. Here we go." They traversed the river, no problem except visible tears running down Alice's cheeks. The other guests made it across with no mishaps.

Bertha felt she needed to lighten the mood so she said, "Good job, ma'am. See. . . that wasn't so bad. Trust your horse. His name is Jocko and he's a seasoned pack tripper; he'll keep you safe. Now let's cowgirl-up and join the others, okay?"

Once they were on the trail things settled down. The trail wound up and down through tranquil forests. A lone moose partially hidden behind some swamp brush watched in curiosity as the trekkers passed. Charlie often startled deer from his lead position; however, they sprinted off the trail and out of sight before the guests saw them.

Stopping just long enough for a short rest, water and cold lunch the group reached Three-Mile-Meadow in good spirits by late afternoon. Mountains rising 9700 feet above sea level flanked both east and west of the meadow, with Eagle Peak at the far south, standing tall at 11300 feet, staring down at them in aloofness. The group would traverse Eagle Peak Pass and down into Yellowstone National Park tomorrow.

Everyone had jobs to do before they could think of supper. Charlie and Larry unpacked the mules and then turned them loose to graze the meadow. A small creek running through the meadow provided water. Bertha "un-tacked" the horses, turning all but two loose to join the mules. She staked Charlie's mustang gelding and Larry's Appy mare close to camp, as they would be used to round up the other animals in the morning. Then she set about arranging the cooking area and making a campfire. Charlie chopped wood for the fire while Larry went to hunt for supper. Game was plentiful in the long meadow, from moose and deer to beavers, muskrats, marmots and hares. John and Albert set up their own tents to help; Louise and Alice gathered kindling wood.

Work helped bring the group together, and

that evening, stomachs filled with rabbits cooked on a spit, beans and biscuits, they sat around the campfire and swapped stories. Louise told of her experience back in Virginia as head mistress of an all-girls school. "I can't wait to relate all my western adventures to the girls when I return teaching next spring," she said.

"You don't have to tell about my foolishness this morning," Alice, now able to joke about her earlier panic in the creek, chimed in.

Albert, it seemed, was president of the Old Dominion Bank in Richmond, and his brother, John, was editor of the *Richmond Tribune*. "I intend to publish a series of articles about our journey by train to Denver, stage to Cody, wagon to Wapiti and now horses through the mountains. It will have great public appeal! Everyone back East is hungry to learn if there are any Indians or bison left and crave tales about Yellowstone and mountain men."

Morning brought ground fog and two young moose playing behind the tents. Bertha left her cooking area to wake the guests so they could watch the moose butt heads and chase each other in the tall grasses.

"Is coffee ready?" Albert asked as he stood by the blazing fire. "Alice would like me to bring her a cup."

"Nope, but the water's boiling; so here, if you want to help, just dump in a handful of these coffee grounds and set the pot aside to simmer. I'll throw an eggshell in to settle the grounds in a minute, then it'll be drinkable.

"Better hurry the others along, too, as eggs and bacon are ready and we need to get an early start over the pass today."

The Eagle Pass trail climbed steeply through forested switchbacks until just before reaching the summit. There, the trail crossed a series of open ledges. Looking down at a 100-foot vertical drop caused most first-timers to become anxious. Alice, not only anxious, was terrified. She whispered, so that Bertha, riding behind her, could hardly hear, "I can't do this . . . I'm scared; I want to get off and walk."

"You cannot do that, ma'am; there is not enough room to dismount," Bertha told her. The trail was only a couple of feet wide—no room to pass in order to lead her across. "You just stop Jocko right where you are and look to your right, up the mountain. When Charlie sees we're not coming, he'll be back and help you across. . . do not look down to your left. Time to cowgirl-up again."

Charlie tied his horse and urged the others to find a shrub and tie-up at the summit. He walked back to the ledges and just short of losing his temper and threatening Alice with bodily harm, said, "Ma'am, stop cryin', hang on and I'll lead ya safely to the top."

They all took a welcomed rest break and enjoyed the vista. Bertha commented to Charlie, "You know, every time I stand here on this summit I feel akin to being an angel in heaven, overlooking other mountains, valleys, rivers and creeks. It's as if the whole world's spread out below us."

"The only thing wrong with that is, you'll never be like an angel, dear," he said with a grin, his previous anger now cooled, "at least not in this lifetime."

"Well, I see you're getting to be your ol' sweet self again. . . welcome back."

"I got angry because I was scared Alice might do somethin' stupid like try to get off, or worse yet, yank on Jocko's mouth tryin' to turn him around. Aw, hell, suppose I ought to go apologize to her; after all, she's from the East and never's been up a western mountain."

"That would be the nice thing to do, dear."

"I'll go talk to her now while you're pretending to be an angel," he smirked.

Feelings soothed, feathers smoothed, they descended to Howell Creek and easier riding. Charlie placed Alice between his pack mules and Larry where she felt cared for and safe, looked after by two strong and handsome mountain men. Her husband smiled to himself. Bertha was relieved to ride behind the trekkers where it was peaceful and quiet again. They were now in Yellowstone Park.

Charlie planned to camp on the Yellowstone River and fish for the legendary Yellowstone cutthroat trout. However, the guests expressed their interest in reaching a campsite—as soon as possible—therefore they camped a few miles before the river along Mountain Creek. Exhausted, the guests retired before sunset while Bertha, Charlie and Larry stayed late by the campfire enjoying the closeness of the stars, the echo of howling wolves and sounds of other night creatures.

Later the next morning, following the Yellowstone River south, Charlie pointed out a female grizzly and her cub climbing the hillside across the river. During their lunch break, Bertha walked along the riverbank and noticed fresh grizzly prints in the sand and a nearby pile of large grizzly scat almost the size of a horse-manure pile.

"I think we'd better hang our food supplies tonight," she remarked to her husband later.

"Yep. I was thinkin' the same thing after we saw that sow and cub this mornin'. The park patrol is recommendin' that all food supplies be hoisted ten feet high between trees whenever we bring guests campin' into Yellowstone. I hear they're considerin' makin' it a park law in the near future. Too many people invadin' grizzly country; don't want the beasts gettin' used to associatin' people with food. Bad for business."

They followed the river valley to a point near the confluence of the Thorofare and Yellowstone Rivers and made camp early. Larry went fishing and brought back cutthroat trout for supper. Around the campfire that night Bertha announced, "We'll layover an extra day here so everyone, including the animals, can rest a spell. It's a beautiful spot to trout fish, hike, relax here in camp or take a bath in the quiet pool over in the shallows of the Thorofare. And you can sleep as late as you want if you don't care about breakfast." The guests smiled at that news.

"There's a history to this valley isn't there?" asked John.

"Yep," Charlie volunteered. "This valley's fourteen miles long and three miles wide. Indians, traders and trappers held their annual 'rendeevu' here for several years before movin' the get-together southwest over near the Tetons. Hundreds partied and palave'd for weeks until all their goods had been traded and money spent. 'Cause it's wide and easy to travel, Indians, fur trappers and mountain men the likes of Jeremiah Johnson, John Colter, William Sublette and Jim Bridger often used the same trail we were on today and may have camped right here where we're at now. There's a small lake just yonder off the Yellowstone, named after Bridger."

"Charlie, that's the most words I ever heard you say at one time," Larry said after the guests tucked in for the night.

Bertha chuckled, "Guess you ain't seen him after a few shots of whisky, have you—talk your ear off without saying a thing of value."

"Ya better watch what you're tellin', ol' lady, or I'll start relatin' some tales about you."

"Go ahead. I'm going to find a buffalo robe and crawl under it. 'Night."

Dawn brought a spectacular sunrise along the Thorofare. Bluing skies and warming sun welcomed the well-rested guests as they crawled out of their bedrolls. A pair of golden eagles circled majestically overhead; trout jumped enticingly in the river—signs of a good day to come.

With no set schedule for the day, the atmosphere was tranquil. The horses and mules came into camp out of habit. Charlie gave them some grain cubes to keep them quiet as he walked among them examining the animals' legs and hooves. He haltered a couple that needed tending to and tied them to nearby trees.

Larry had shot a young doe that morning and was digging a ground pit in which he would cook a venison roast for supper. They would pack the remaining carcass for future meals.

Albert and John went hiking to check out Bridger Lake east of camp. Louise had washed some delicates in the river and was draping them over bushes to dry. Bertha decided to join Alice, who was sitting on a large rock at the river's edge. "Howdy, cowgirl. How are you doing today?"

"You know, I don't remember ever being this relaxed and content. I'm real sorry for being a problem guest and irritating like a burr under a saddle at times; however, I'm going to take pleasure in this piece of heaven here by the Thorofare, and from this day forward I promise to cowgirl-up, as you say and enjoy the remainder of the trek.

"Are we going to climb more mountains?" Alice asked hesitantly.

Bertha smiled at the lady's courage, resolve and timidity. "We haven't decided our return route yet, but I think we can find an easier trail than the one we came in on."

"Oh, thank you. I do enjoy riding and sightseeing; it's just that I've never climbed mountains on horseback—but, I'm determined to ride wherever we have to, without complaining, from here on."

That evening, after the guests had retired to their tents, Bertha related this conversation to Charlie. "She's determined to be a real trooper, but I don't think she could handle the Rampart . . . so why don't we pack the alternate route following Pass Creek up to the Ishawooa? Then it's an easy trek to the South Fork."

"I agree. Albert asked me this afternoon if we could take the shortest, easiest route back. He said he and John had seen and done more than they expected, and he's concerned about his wife. She didn't want to come on the trip but he talked her into it. Now he's thinking maybe that was a bad idea."

"She'll be okay," Bertha added, "though I expect she'll be some happy to be back sleeping on a feather bed, between cotton sheets, in a couple days!"

Come morning, Charlie told the guests about their travel plans: "It'll be a long but easy day's ride today. We'll climb over one more mountain with a nice view and no ledges, then we'll make camp on the other side. It's elk country so keep your eyes open and your talk soft."

Alice rode relaxed and with a smile, chatting with Louise about the mountain flora and fauna along the trail and asking questions—too many, according to Bertha who trailed the ladies. "Is that mountain phlox?" Alice asked. "Do Indians use the Indian paintbrush?" Louise wanted to know. "What do elk eat?" And on and on.

Finally, having reached her social limit, Bertha said politely, "If you want to see some elk today, you'd better be looking more and talking less until we get to our campsite."

They had just begun climbing switchbacks when Charlie stopped the team and pointed right—there on the far slope was a herd of 30 elk grazing, cows, calves and a magnificent bull. They watched the trekkers but did not move off. After a spell, the team continued up the mountain, with the guests hoping to see more.

As they crossed the somewhat level crest, a thunderstorm threatened. Bertha said, "Hold up ladies. You might want to get off and don your slickers; it looks like rain ahead, and there's no proper place to dismount once we begin the descent."

The men had halted also and were putting on their slickers.

Within minutes the sky opened up, winds blew cold rain, lightening flashed and thunder boomed. The trail became slippery—the topsoil turning to greasy mud making it difficult for the animals to keep their footing, many times sliding on all four feet at once. After negotiating a particularly steep turn of a switchback, Bertha called to Alice, "Hey cowgirl. How're you doing so far?"

"So far, so good," was her remote response. "Do you ever stop and wait out a storm?"

"Nope. Have to make camp in time to set up before dark. Hang in there; you're doing fine."

"Okay," Alice replied. "I was just wondering."

Halfway down the mountain the rain stopped, clouds passed and sunshine appeared, as did smiles on the guests' faces. Luckily, the packs had time to dry before reaching camp in the Ishawooa Valley. The site was not even damp, since the rain had been limited to the mountains, as were many such storms in the Rockies.

Seven horses, five mules, twenty-four thundering hooves coming down the valley into camp woke the guests the next morning. The animals had strayed during the night causing Larry and Charlie to ride three miles one way to find them and bring them in. It gave Bertha time to pick berries she added to the hotcakes she was preparing for this last day on the trail.

The aroma of hotcakes, eggs and bacon frying permeated the air drawing guests out of their tents. "I think I'm getting used to riding all day, up and down mountains and across rivers. I feel real good today," Alice said all bubbly and smiles.

"That's because you know we're nearing the end of our trip and you won't have to sleep on the ground tomorrow, or get soaked in the rain," her husband chided her.

"And I can use an outhouse," chimed in the usually quiet Louise, flushing a bit.

It was a perfect day for the guests' last ride, following the creek to the South Fork and then north to Bill Cody's TE ranch on the Shoshone. No traumatic mountain trails, ledges to cross, or inclement weather to contend with—only scattered herds of bison peacefully grazing the hillsides along the river valley. Great way to end a trip.

"My words can't justly express what an outstanding excursion you gave us," exclaimed Albert when it was time to say good-bye. "My life's outlook has changed for having gone with you. Thank you very much."

"I am going to put it all down on paper; it'll make for wonderful tales in the *Richmond Tribune*," John said enthusiastically. "And, I add my thanks to my brothers."

"I must say that it was a once-in-a-lifetime adventure for me, and I thank you for it," Louise said with genuine sincerity.

"Thank you so much for putting up with me and getting me back safely," Alice said with tears in her eyes. "I'll always remember this experience and hope to be a better person for it." She gave them all hugs, even Bertha, who bristled a bit but endured.

As the outfit departed for Cody, Bertha was still sputtering. "I ain't never been hugged by no woman afore."

"Well then, guess this trip will be memorable for you, too, won't it dear?" her husband teased.

WILD HORSES

Upon returning to Cody from a recent horse pack trip into the lower east corner of Yellowstone Park, Bertha and Charlie Daye hurried into their favorite bar at the Irma Hotel to tip back a few shots of whiskey.

Bertha, long on aggression and short on tolerance, said, "I wonder if all eastern dudes wanting to experience a bit of our west will be as delicate as those four guests of Buffalo Bill's? If so, maybe we'd better be rethinking taking guests pack tripping into the mountains . . . that sure was trying on my patience."

Usually the quiet one, Charlie's tongue began to loosen with drink. "Ya done fine, honey. I wasn't sure for a while whether Lady Alice was gonna make it back to Bill's ranch without havin' another bout of the vapors. Ya musta done some real sweet talkin' for her to give ya a hug whilst we was sayin' our fare-the-wells," Charlie said with a grin.

"Ol' man," she said as she smacked him, nearly knocking him off his barstool, "that was none of *my* doing. She was just thankful to get back in one piece that's all." Easily riled, she continued, "Now *that* subject is closed. You hear me! I don't want it brought up again, 'specially not in public.

"I'm going to clean up before we go to the government office to check on work, and you should, too. You stink worse'n a bear been hibernating all winter," she said stomping up the stairs to a waiting tub of hot water.

When she met her husband later in the hotel bar, whistles abounded until she gave her "don't mess with me" glare. "Ya sure are a looker when you get all gussied up, Bertha. Ya got more 'n half these hombres steppin' on their tongues wishin' ya was theirs, and the rest are so drunk they cain't see straight."

"Flattery like that'll get you anywhere, ol' man. You don't look so bad yourself—cleaned up and all. Let's hurry and get our business done with that government agent, then come back and check out that featherbed upstairs," she said, giving him a wink.

Charlie had married Bertha when she was no more than sixteen and running from a cruel and dishonest uncle. Despite their age difference, they had been loyal partners in life—and on the trail—since. He, an aging, albeit handsome, lanky outfitter who loved his mules and mountains; she, an attractive, feisty and hard working horsewoman.

They arrived at the government office looking for Mr. Grady. He dispensed assignments to them from time to time. Their last was scouting what remained of small bison herds down on the South Fork of the Shoshone.

"Hi Charlie, Bertha," he said, shaking hands with them both. "Nice to see you again."

"Same here, Mr. Grady," Charlie said.

"What can I do for you today?"

"Heard you might have some work for us," Bertha said. "We just come in from taking some of Bill Cody's eastern guests into the Yellowstone and Thorofare area."

"Seems like all them easterners want a taste of the West these days. How'd that go?"

"It was quite an experience for them—and us. Think we'd sooner scout wolves or count buffalo." They all laughed.

"Well, maybe what I have in mind is just what you'd like then. The government says they would like an estimate of the number of wild horses roaming the Pryor Mountains in the Crow reservation, thinking to take on a program of catching and taming them for cavalry use.

"And, speaking of wolves, as the bison herds have all but been eliminated, they are migrating west from the plains in search of a primary food source. A sizeable pack has zeroed in on range cattle and the Tillett family, north of Lovell, is complaining loudly. Seems they are losing cattle every month, so feel free to shoot wolves if you see any along the way.

"The Tilletts also expressed an interest in the plight of the wild horses and are willing to supply men if you need extra help."

"We could use a couple of hands; Larry Motts has worked with us, but he signed on with another outfit this mornin'," Charlie said.

"The Tilletts' TX Ranch runs along Crooked Creek, which is on the trail to the Pryors. Bill and Bessie Tillett said you're welcome to stay the night, re-supply, and pick up more men; whatever you need. . . they'll help."

"Do you want us to bring back horses or just count them?" Bertha asked.

"Good horseflesh fetches a high price these days, as I'm sure you know, Bertha. Ft. Reno, Oklahoma, is becoming a remount station for the military and is known for its horse breeding and training programs. They might be interested in sending some cavalry north to check the quality of the Pryor mustangs if you bring back a few. You could then sell them or keep them for yourself—up to you."

Before they left Mr. Grady's office, they learned that the last estimate of horses running in the entire Crow reservation, done a decade earlier, was ten thousand. They had their work cut out for them.

Three days later, Charlie, riding a new pinto gelding, leading a pack mule, followed by Bertha, riding her favorite red-chestnut gelding, Flame, left Cody heading northeast past Heart Mountain on toward the Pryor Mountains.

This had been Bertha's home ground for a while before meeting Charlie, when she had escaped from her drunken uncle to the west side of the Bighorns. However, she loved the land: the rough ridges laced with ponderosa, cottonwood-lined gulches and creeks, and grassy meadows winding through the long serene valley. Their route took them past wind-carved outcrops that harbored hundreds of birds' nests and had sheltered her when she had stolen a horse and run away from her uncle.

She had spent three weeks in and out of hidey-holes where she had retreated at night, during storms or in drastic drops of temperature. Some were animal dens full of scat; others were overhanging ledges. Some were nothing but juniper or willow thickets she and her horses could push into to get out of harsh weather. Then Charlie came to her rescue; she would never forget.

Waking her out of her reverie, Charlie said, "We're almost there."

They rode up the twisting rutted road that led to the TX Ranch buildings nestled under a protective ridge. Bill Tillett strolled down the porch steps to greet them. He wore his hair so short you could not see it from under his wide Stetson. His build was strong, his face weathered, as were his hands as he reached to shake theirs.

"Welcome to the TX Ranch, Mr. and Mrs. Daye."

"Please, it's Charlie and Bertha," she said.

"Please ta meet ya, Mr. Tillett," Charlie added.

"It's Bill, and this is my dear wife, Bessie, right here." She nodded to them as she walked up beside her husband.

"I heard from Mr. Grady you'd be passing this way soon. You can put your animals in that empty corral over there and store your gear in the barn. There's water in the trough."

"We're about to eat," said Bessie. "We'd be pleased if you'd join us."

"That would be much appreciated, ma'am.

We'll be in as soon's we're done takin' care of things."

"Name's *Bessie*, not Ma'am," she said smiling.

Bessie was a slight-built woman who had once been a Texas beauty. Their ranch's first herd of cattle was purchased by Bessie's father, Frank Strong from Amarillo, and the right hip brand "TX"—which was his—was never changed by the Tilletts.

After supper, sitting on the log porch sipping good whiskey, Bill said, "Mr. Grady mentioned you might like a couple of our hands to go along with you. Are you hunting wolves or searching for wild horses?"

"Well, both, I guess. We've been hired to estimate the number of wild horses rangin' in the Pryors and to shoot wolves if we come across any. You havin' some trouble with 'em?"

"Yes. . . more than usual. Most remaining buffalo have relocated to Yellowstone, and the wolf packs are moving west from the Dakotas in search of food. A large pack of about seven, that we've seen, has taken to killing our cattle, and we've found numerous wild foal skeletons picked clean by scavengers but probably killed by wolves. Found some paw prints. Not cats. Wolves for sure.

"Bessie and I are *most* anxious about losing

our cattle. However, we've grown to love watching the wild horses roam this area—they were here prior to our building this ranch a decade ago—and we don't want to lose them to wolves, or the government either. So you see our concern is three-fold: cattle, wolves and mustangs," Bill said.

"Well, our job is with the wild horses, and from what I hear, there are enough to keep us tabulatin' for a few weeks or more, so we won't have time to wolf hunt, but we sure will keep an eye out for 'em and shoot what we can."

"That's all I'm asking, Charlie. I told two of my young cowboys, Duke and Marlon, to pack a mule; they're to help you for a couple of weeks. After that, we need them back here for branding and castrating calves."

"Sounds good. We'll be leavin' 'round sunup in the mornin' then. Thanks for your hospital'ty."

Bessie said, "Sorry we don't have room for y'all in here—we're planning to expand—but until then, there's room at the end of the barn, if that's okay."

"Sure, we'll be fine," said Bertha, "and thanks for the meal. Good night."

Sunup found the four riders and two pack mules following Crooked Creek, passing a multitude of cottonwoods, box elders and willows on their way into the Crow reservation and Pryor Mountains.

"Charlie, do you have a plan to find and count the wild horses?" Bertha asked as she rode up beside him.

"Yep."

"Come on, ol' man. Remember I'm your partner. Talk to me."

"Well, I thought we'd first ride up the canyons of the Bighorn River. . . then make a big sweep north to west around the mountains. . . then tighten our circle and see how we're doing from there."

"Okay; sounds like a good plan," she said, still a bit disgruntled.

They spotted their first group of horses within the first hour of riding. The band (small herd) consisted of one bay stallion six dark mares, eleven younger stock between a year and two years old and six foals. They were all black-based colors of blue and red roan, bay, brown, black, gray-striped grulla and dun.

As the riders neared, they noted the mustangs' heads were medium length with a broad, flat forehead and wide-set eyes. They looked on the smaller side of average riding horses (14.2 hands, one hand = 4 inches), although sturdy and well balanced.

As the riders ventured farther into the Crow reservation, seeing groups of 15 to 75 horses every couple of hours, they noted the narrow front placement of their legs and well-developed heart girth, giving them an unusually smooth gait. Bertha commented, "I'll bet they have incredible stamina, Charlie, and they look comfortable to ride because they don't waste energy bouncing around. Let's bring a chosen few back with us. Whaddaya think?"

"Okay, just so's we wait until we're about done countin'. I trust your judgment on horseflesh; you're the expert."

That night, laying on bedrolls under the starlit skies, wolf howls and other sounds from night creatures serenaded them to sleep.

The next day, during a mid-morning break, Marlon found the carcass of a foal in a dense stand of chokecherry in a draw. There wasn't much left of the newborn; wolves and a few lesser predators, coyotes, crows, and anything else with a taste for flesh, had reduced it to a chewed-on skull, scattered bones and hide.

He called the others and pointed to paw prints left in the dry sand, partly blown away but still identifiable. Front paws wide, with claw prints visible. Rear paws more diamond-shaped, claws also visible. These were not the round, wide and clawless prints of a cat—

mountain lion—they were definitely wolf.

"Wolves, sure 'nuf," said Charlie.

"Looks like it," Duke and Marlon agreed.

"I'd like to shoot the varmints," Bertha said.

"If ya keep your eyes peeled, ya just might get your chance," Charlie said.

They rode as silently as they could for the next few miles down a dry gulch, glancing periodically up at the rims on either side. Charlie, leading the group, held up his hand to stop, then pointed up the ridge. He'd spotted four wolves sunning themselves atop a ledge about 300 yards up the north rim. Putting his finger to his lips to indicate quiet, he unsheathed his rifle and pointed to the others to do the same. Using hand signs only, Charlie held up four fingers, pointed to the wolves and pointed to each of the four riders. He indicated he would take the first one, Bertha the second, Duke the third and Marlon the fourth. They all aimed, Charlie shot first and other three shots followed. The wolves lay still.

"Looks to be a den about a 50 feet upslope and to the west," Charlie said. "I wonder if there's pups in there."

Duke asked, "Do you want me to ride up and check?"

"No. We don't have time to mess with wolves. If there's pups, hopefully we killed the mother and that should be the end of them too. At least there's four less of 'em now."

They left the canyon areas after two days and rode northwest up ridges with spectacular sweeping views of valleys, gorges, ravines and chasms. "Wow!" exclaimed Bertha after reaching the summit of one ridge. "I can see four different herds. With that spyglass, Charlie you can count them from here. All I see are masses of horses."

They counted six herds, ranging from 50 to 150 horses each, that day. Their total was already up to 2000 head.

The next few days proved the same: riding rims and ridges covered with conifers, grassy valleys, gorges and gulches and counting wild horses. They spotted elk and big horn sheep in the high mountain elevations, mule and white-tailed deer and antelope on the lower slopes. No shortage of game. The riders feasted on venison nightly.

On their tenth day out, they encountered three Crow Indians at one of the animal watering holes. They were riding mountain mustangs. One, David Black Horse, spoke English. Charlie told him they were counting wild horses on the mountains and surrounding area and said, "We've counted eight thousand like yours. Are they good horses?"

David Black Horse sat taller and puffed out his chest, saying, "The best. Run fast. Run long." (Bertha listened intently.) When asked about the number of horses ranging throughout their reservation that were not on the Pryor Mountains, David Black Horse answered, "As many as are in the mountains, there are on the plains also. We have plenty horses; for many, many years they have been here."

After complimenting the Crows on their fine animals and thanking them for their information, Charlie guided the group up to an old abandoned silver mine where they could rest their horses as he devised a plan. He sat quietly for a while and then said, "I'm thinkin' we're near completin' the inner circle. . . maybe three more days. From here on, Bertha, ya look over the small bachelor bands real good and we'll be scoutin' us a small ravine where we can drive horses into a corner and rope us a few good ones—after we've completed countin', that is."

Two days later, Bertha exclaimed, "There, in that valley below. There are three nice-looking young stallions grazing one end and a small family band at the other. I'm going down alone to take a closer look."

"Okay," Charlie said. "We'll wait for ya here."

Bertha was a natural horsewoman with

an uncanny ability to understand and communicate with horses. She tied Flame to a low-branched ponderosa and descended to the valley floor until she was within 20 yards of the three bachelors. There was a black and a bay with fine coats and a gray roan with a wavy coat and kinky mane and tail. They all exhibited the broad flat forehead with a long and silky forelock, and soft, almond-shaped, expressive eyes. Their muzzles were narrow and refined; ears set deep and alert to her every move. Their crescent-shaped nostrils expanded, smelling her scent in the air. Their slightly crested necks, accented with long, silky manes, were medium length, proportioned to size and inserted well into their shoulders, which were long and sloping to the natural slant of their pasterns. They had well-defined withers with a smooth transition from their necks to their backs. *What magnificent horses,* she thought.

Bertha returned to her horse and continued riding to the far end of the valley to observe the family band. The golden-colored alpha mare spotted her while she was still several hundred yards away, and the black stallion leader warned her to keep her distance with a loud, shrill whinny. The other band members became instantly alert. There were two bay mares and three frisky foals: one, light reddish, and the other two, dark. Their conformation was similar to the bachelors', probably the same family.

Bertha returned to the others, face flushed, words spilling out too fast. "I want them . . . or some of them. . . they are gorgeous!"

"OK, then, let's finish up countin' tomorrow; then we'll return and see what we can plan for capturing a few," Charlie said.

"Duke, are you and Marlon in for a roundup, of sorts?"

"Sure," said Duke, not mentioning he had never been party to one.

"I'm game," chimed in Marlon. "Haven't had me a roundup in a couple of years."

* * *

Roundup day. The riders worked together and plugged one end of a narrow ravine, off the valley floor. Their plan was to run the two bunches together and then head them into the ravine, closing the makeshift gate they had built from downed ponderosas and cut junipers. If they roped their choice horses at once, then let the remaining free again, it would be less chaotic and over quickly. With one end cut and sharpened they had pounded four posts into the ground in various spots to secure the roped horses until they settled down.

The plan worked like clockwork until the mustangs were confined—too many stallions in too close quarters—and all hell broke loose as a band stallion leader began fighting with one of the young bachelor stallions.

"Let's get in there—fast—and get a rope on whatever horse you want. Then snub 'em good so you don't lose 'em when the rest go free," Bertha yelled over the noise of whinnying, squealing, snorting and stomping.

"I want the palomino mare; Charlie, can you rope the black colt for me?" Taking charge, she said, "Let's go boys."

Pandemonium ensued. Marlon roped the gray colt; Charlie roped the young black; Bertha roped the golden mare, trying to keep her reddish foal near her at the same time. Duke tried twice to rope the young bay stallion fighting the leader but lost his concentration, and thus his aim, as the black band stallion turned on him. The others snubbed their horses and ran to help.

Bertha yelled, "Marlon, get the gate open, quick," as she stepped between the black and Duke, swinging her lariat round and round to keep the stallion's attention off Duke, who was sprawled on the ground. Charlie hauled Duke out of the way just in time to avoid the frenzied two stallions, two mares and three foals as they dashed out the gate to freedom. Then, in answer to her dam's frantic whinny, the light reddish foal hesitantly returned to her side.

Whew! That was exciting, Bertha thought as she sagged against the makeshift gate. The men made their way over to inspect their catch. Recovering, she walked to where they were standing and admired the glistening and nervous mustangs. Still giving orders, she said, "Let's move *real* slow, boys; talk softly and see if they'll quiet down. Duke, you haul some water and feed in here. Marlon, close the gate again. Charlie and I will loosen the snubs in a few minutes but still keep them tied for a while longer."

While the men set up camp, Bertha continued to stay in the makeshift corral with the horses . . . standing, sitting, singing softly, walking slowly, and kneeling down to the foal's level to let the filly sniff. She would wait until she got back to their log cabin and corrals on the North Fork of the Shoshone before she'd gentle and train them. Meanwhile, she would work quietly around them, getting them to trust her and not be frightened. Already she had made a makeshift rope halter for the mare and slipped it on her without being bitten or driven off and befriended the filly, figuring it would show the mare that her intentions were good and would be an easy way to gain the mare's trust. She would not attempt to gentle the black until

Charlie gelded him back at their homestead.

She figured the black colt was around three years old; the other gray colt appeared younger. Although the mare looked in good health, Bertha would not be able to tell the age until she could check the mare's teeth. The filly, she named Sunset, was no more than four months old.

They relaxed the remainder of the day to rest their horses and summarize their wild horse count. Charlie's final tally showed 11,450 horses grazing on and around the Pryor Mountains, and if David Black Horse could be believed, another 10,000 to 12,000 northeast of the mountain on the Crow reservation. That would please the U.S. Cavalry looking for new mounts.

The Tillett family could rest a little easier with four fewer wolves to kill their cattle. Duke and Marlon could go back to the den and check for pups, or more adults, if Bill wanted to eliminate the whole pack.

* * *

Heading back to Cody, Charlie led the young black, Bertha led the palomino mare with her foal frolicking close beside her; Marlon led the gray colt, while Duke led the mules, his body slumped, his head down. He was young; he would soon recover his pride, and thanks to Bertha's and Charlie's quick actions, he would live to try his hand at capturing wild horses another day.

WINNER TAKES ALL

After counting wild horses on the Crow reservation for the U.S. government last fall, Bertha and Charlie Daye stayed the winter at their homestead on the North Fork of the Shoshone west of Cody, Wyoming. He was now in his forties and still loved mules and the mountains. Always an excellent horsewoman, she was now in her early thirties and had grown more outspoken as her husband became more reticent. Together they made a good team.

In between guiding hunters into the high country, they had spent their off hours gentling and training the four mustangs they had brought back from the reservation. The palomino mare and especially her sorrel foal, now a yearling, had been easy to gentle with just a few corral lessons. Being ponied on the three-day trek back from the Pryor Mountains had helped gain their trust and cooperation.

The Tilletts' wrangler, Marlon, had gelded the gray and then turned him over to Bertha when he accepted a job in Cheyenne for the winter. Named Greystone, the now three-year-old turned out to be spirited but willing and trainable. This spring Bertha was riding him on the trail. However, the black, now four-years-old, was another matter.

Bertha had intended to have Charlie geld him upon their return. However, his superior conformation, intelligence and agility persuaded them to keep him a stallion for breeding, at least for a while. To get maximum use from him, Bertha planned to break him to ride as well. He had other ideas. Proud and handsome, she had named him Washakie and although she liked and admired his spirit and independence, she also found him arrogant, willful, sometimes cooperative, and always testing her. He was not going to give up his dominance easily.

"Charlie, if he'd only be consistent, I could deal with him. The bugger is willing to have me ride him at a walk, jog and lope around the corral one day, and the next, he bucks the instant I mount. . . so I return to making him run and turn until he faces me and accepts me as his boss again. He's good for the next few days; then he has another uncooperative spell, and I start all over. Luckily, he's not mean or I'd have him cut."

"I just don't know. . ." she said in frustration.

"I've watched you two, and I know mules better 'n horses, but I'd say he's just playin' games and havin' fun getting ya frustrated. Maybe ya need to introduce somethin' new or challengin' so he'll stop thinkin' about bestin' ya."

"I think you're right, ol' man. He knows his gaits and cues to turn and stop, so I guess it's time to take him out of the small corral into a larger, but still fenced, area like the winter pastures where he can experience nature with me on his back. I'll do that tomorrow. . . that is, if you'll plan to be on hand."

"I'll be in the background, dear, just like always. Don't want anythin' untoward happenin' to ya; who'd be bossin' me around if'n ya wasn't here?" Charlie asked with affection.

"Just remember that ol' man." She smiled and winked.

Bertha always gave the black his time, running the small pen with the saddle cinched and stirrups flapping, to let him get out his bucks, kicks and kinks before mounting. She had been training him with a rawhide bosal hackamore and decided that introducing the bit today would only add confusion. New territory would be enough to pique his interest without worrying about new equipment.

She mounted and jogged him a few times around the corral, then signaled Charlie to open the gate. Washakie's ears pricked up as he pranced through the gate into the pasture. It was fenced with three strands of barbed wire, which stood four feet aboveground. Compared to their summer pasture of one hundred acres, the five acres was a small area. He, however, mistakenly thought he was free on open range again. His nostrils flared and Bertha felt his anxiety. Instead of holding him in, she let him jog, thinking he would be more comfortable on the move rather than confined to a walk. His gait was steady so she let him out a little more, into a lope. That was all he needed to encourage his wild instinct. He snorted, shook his head and launched himself first into a hand gallop and then into racing mode, as he quickly covered ground to the far side of the pasture.

Bertha thought, *Oh no; fence coming up, won't stop, won't turn, intent on racing straight ahead—disaster looming.* She was about to bail off when she felt him gather himself. . . and he flew, as if lifted by wings, over the fence and landed on the ground, moving at a speed no less than a runaway train.

Charlie watched in dread as his wife, astride the black, headed straight toward the far fence line. He began running in their direction not wanting to think of the catastrophe that was about to happen. Then he stopped in amazement, as she and the black cleared the fence by more than two feet. He turned back to the barn where he hurried to saddle his big buckskin, taking chase after them as fast as his horse could run, while shaking his head and thinking, *Bertha, you're in for one heckuva ride; I sure hope ya survive this day.*

Washakie was flying over the ground, up steep slopes, down into ravines and up the other side, leaping sagebrush and having the time of his life, headed west toward home. Fortunately, for Bertha, the town of Cody was between them and the Crow reservation. *I'll just hang on 'til then; he'll slow down in time,* she hoped. Just outside of Cody, near the construction site of the work-in-process Shoshone dam, he did slow down, partly out of anticipation of civilization and partly because he'd just covered five miles at a runaway gallop and needed to catch his second wind. Bertha regained control and reined him to a walk and after a few minutes she halted. She did not know whose heart pounded faster, the black's or hers. *Wow,* she thought, *I've ridden horses almost all thirty years of my life, but I've never ridden like that.*

She wanted to dismount, hug her horse and have a good cry, but she was afraid she might not being able to hang on to him from the ground, so she settled for stroking his neck and crooning to him. "Washakie," she soothed as she patted his sweaty neck. "You are some kinda horseflesh, boy. If only I could learn to control you," she added.

Charlie met them within a couple of miles after they had turned around and were walking back home. "I'm glad to see you're still on his back and in once piece. You okay?" he asked apprehensively. Pretty as she was, he had learned over the past ten years not to treat Bertha as a fragile flower; she was a tough lady. Not that he didn't worry about her, she just didn't like him to make a big deal of emotional situations—like now.

"If I get off, Charlie, will you help hold the black? I need to get my feet on the ground and stop my legs from shaking for a bit."

"Sure, he's pretty much calmed down after that run, and Bucky's here to keep him comp'ny; he'll be okay now."

As she came over and gave him a big hug, she said, "In all my years, I ain't ever ridden a horse like that one, Charlie. Wow, is all I can say; well not all—he sure can run, and jump. Did you see him fly over that fence, Charlie?"

"Yes, dear. He took near six feet of air. I don't want to see ya doin' that again soon; had me plumb worried 'til I seen ya land and keep moving. That's the mustang in him, surefooted and fearless."

On the way back home, they chatted about various ways, and training techniques, to control Washakie on the trail. Bertha mentioned that the black would be a good match in a race against their friend Buffalo Bill Cody's famous white Arabian horse, McKinley. Bertha had tried unsuccessfully to beg, buy or negotiate for Bill's stallion for years; maybe she could win him in a wager on a horse race.

Charlie thought this was a bad idea. "It'd be a losin' situation, dear. *If* we beat Bill's horse, we'd lose a friend; and *if* we lost the race, we'd lose a good horse that has the potential to be a money-makin' breedin' stallion."

"Okay; you're right," she conceded. "But, I'd sure like to race someone, somewhere; I've never seen or ridden a horse that can run like Washakie."

To avoid further confrontation, Charlie uttered his usual, "Yes dear."

* * *

Opportunity presented itself on their next trip into town for supplies. A poster pinned to the door of the feed and grain store read:

WANTED,
horses to enter
Cody's 4th of July 1903
Stampede Race
10 miles cross-country
Must enter by June 15 – Fee $75
WINNER TAKES ALL
See Slim at the Irma

"I want to enter Washakie. He can win, Charlie; I know he can. Whaddya think?"

"Women don't ride in horse races, Bertha and I sure ain't ridin' the black. I'm a mule and mount'in man, remember."

"*I'll* ride," she retorted stubbornly.

"Okay, *if* ya decide to ride, I'll support ya, but there's a couple of things ya need to be considerin': one, we'd have to sacrifice a month's pay to cover the entrance fee, and two, the black definitely needs a lot more trainin' on bein' cooperative."

"But look at the money—'Winner Takes All'," she countered. "And I've got four weeks, 28 days, to train. I'll work with him every day."

They stopped at the Irma Hotel on their way out of town and paid the entrance fee, registering him as "Washakie, owned by Charlie and Bertha Daye." No rider's name given. Fifteen horses were already signed up, with two weeks left to enter.

Bertha became a serious racehorse trainer; her reputation and a month's wages were at stake. No more bosal. She settled on a bit with just a slight port because the black did not have a hard mouth; she just needed some leverage if he decided to run again. The bit had long shanks and a slot for a curb chain that, along with more training, should enable her to have the control she needed to quell his willful disposition. She trained him daily, at first with Charlie and Bucky riding alongside, introducing him to buckboards, mule teams, gunshots, wooden bridges and other man-made obstacles that he had not encountered in the wild. Then as he grew to trust her, she rode him alone, with Charlie a half mile behind—just in case. She also rode him at a controlled pace through creeks, up mountains, down craggy ravines and across ledges. He was a natural at these.

Four weeks later, they were a team. Bertha announced, "We're ready to race."

A concerned Charlie and a confident Bertha rode into town before sunup the day before the race so no one would be around to check out the black. They secured two stalls at Cody's west end stock pens: a corner stall to house the black, trying to keep him away from the chaos the middle stalls would bring, and another for themselves set up next to the black.

They met with the other 24 entrants at the Irma at noon. Buffalo Bill Cody himself handed out riding numbers—they were number 16—and briefed everyone about the stampede race schedule. At seven the next morning they were to parade down the center of town so gamblers could see the horses and riders, thus increasing the wagering. At nine o'clock, the race would begin east of Cody, head toward Powell, go around Heart Mountain and return, with the finish line this side of the wooden bridge crossing the Shoshone. There was a catch, however; if a rider wanted, he could take an alternate route on the Cody side of the mountain, crossing some extremely rough ground, ravines and the river. Bertha did not intend to take this route as she was sure Washakie could outrun the other horses and would not need to chance unknown terrain, even if it did cut off two miles.

So far, no one had noticed the black, much less, knew Bertha was riding.

After the meeting, Buffalo Bill tried to corner his friends to get some inside knowledge about their horse named "Washakie" and who was riding, but they slyly disappeared out the back door and returned to keep "The Black" company. They planned to have one of them always around in case he caused trouble. Come suppertime, Bertha left to catch a bite to eat at the Silver Dollar Saloon; Charlie had the first watch. Three cowboys, having had too much to drink in too short a time, were standing around the corner checking out the black. When they got bolder, came closer and proceeded to heckle him, Charlie recognized one of them as the rider of the town's favorite horse to win.

"Hey, old man. Nice horse, but he can't race if you can't ride, now can he?" one of the drunken cowboys said as he grabbed Charlie and threw him against the wood fence. The second cowboy pinned Charlie's arms behind him while the third punched him in the stomach, sending Charlie crumpling to the ground.

They were about to kick and stomp on him when they heard, "*Stop! I'm* riding the black, and *I'm* shooting on the count of three if you're not out of my eyesight by then." They stared down the barrel of a rifle held by a good-looking, but very angry woman. They ran.

"Charlie, honey, you alright?" Bertha sobbed, as she hugged and kissed him.

"Keep that up, dear, and it'll be worth bein' punched just to be tended to by you," he said as he held her close.

Her composure returning she told him, "You

go get something to eat; I'm staying right here with my rifle pointing at anyone who comes near."

While Charlie was at the Silver Dollar, he placed a bet of $35 on the black. Their odds had changed to thirty to one since word was out a woman was riding, an angry one at that.

Washakie danced, pranced and sidestepped, with sweat running freely off his glistening body as he paraded down Cody's main street, nervous as a jackrabbit in a den of coyotes. Charlie had to resort to ponying him beside Bucky to help Bertha keep the black under control—unfortunately, they had not exposed him to "people noises" and crowds.

The parade was coming to the end when a bunch of young boys jumped out in front of Bertha and the black, yelling, "bang, bang, bang" and waving fake rifles at them. That was more than the black could take; he reared up and came down on his front end as his back legs went high in the air. . . Bertha hit the ground amidst the crowd's laughter and jeering: "If you cain't stay on him, howya gonna race him?" and "Go home, woman; bake bread, have kids." Bertha remounted, humiliated but still confident in her horse's ability, and her own, to win the race—if she could stay on.

The starter was their friend Bill Cody. As he

announced the name of each horse and rider, Bertha tried to stay calm so her horse would not feed off her anxiety; she kept Washakie walking in circles to keep his mind occupied. Then Bill announced the crowd to stand back and fired his gun to start the race—at that very moment, she and the black were facing the opposite direction.

"Easy does it," Bertha whispered to the black as he spun around and lunged after the racers. "We've got plenty of time to catch them, boy."

They passed the tail-end horses effortlessly and, within a mile, had passed several more. Riding to catch the pack of eight front-runners, two riders whom she recognized as two of cowboys who beat up Charlie the night before, blocked her way. Fueled by fury, she tried to pass on the right, only to have them pull to the right in front of her; she reined the black to the left and was blocked there, also. She'd either have to circle way around them or. . . Just then, one of the riders swerved to avoid a sage bush; she quickly pressed Washakie with both legs and he cleared the bush, landing between the riders. The cowboys looked at her with recognition and began squeezing her, bumping her horse. When that did not discourage her, one whipped her horse with the ends of his reins while the other tried to kick her foot out of the stirrup and push her off. She regained her balance, leaned over the black's neck and whispered, "Go, Washakie, go."

He responded and left the two cowboys eating dust. However, she had lost precious time in the scuffle, and she could no longer see the front-runners. *Maybe we need to take the alternative route and stay away from the other riders, and trouble,* she thought. She guided the black to the left, leaving the trail to find their way across unknown terrain to the river. The black ran effortlessly, covering rock-strewn ledges as well as desert-like sand. This was his natural running environment. He never broke stride as he sailed over a deep but narrow gully wash, clearing the six-foot space with ease. Then she reined him to a walk and observed a deep ravine with a rider sprawled on the ground at the bottom.

She cautiously made her way to the base and began dismounting when the young man said, "No, keep riding. Rattler spooked my horse. My ankle may be broken but I'll be alright; just send somebody back when you get to town."

"OK. I'll send help."

"Thanks and good luck, lady. Fine horse; hope you win."

"Me too," she yelled over her shoulder as they galloped to the other side of the gorge. Climbing the crest with the sure-footedness of her mustang's heritage, she spotted the river with the main trail on the other side. She crossed at a point where the Shoshone ran swift but not deep, stopping just long enough to let her horse take a few sips of water before continuing onto the well-trodden trail back to Cody.

Then she heard the thunder of pounding hooves as five horses and riders rounded the bend to her right. "This is it, boy," she said to the black as she urged him into a gallop, bringing him in behind the pack. She outdistanced two of the racers as the other three spurred their horses and pulled ahead. With the wooden bridge coming into view, it was time to race—to see just how fast he could run with competition egging him on.

She leaned over his neck, hanging onto his mane, saying, "Go Washakie, go," feeling his strong muscles and long strides take him past one after the other. Tears from the wind spilled from her eyes, blurring her vision as they raced the lead horse across the bridge to the finish line.

She won. By a full head, they crossed the finish line in front of the town's favorite racehorse. Charlie was there to catch and comfort both Bertha and the black.

Losers lodged complaints for allowing a woman to ride. However race official Bill Cody announced: "Wyoming women were granted the legal right to vote in 1869, seems they'd have a legal right to horse race in 1903, if they want."

He congratulated his friends, shaking hands with Charlie and hugging Bertha, saying, "I placed my bets on Washakie once I found out you were riding; made quite a stack of easy money thanks to you and that fine horse."

"Suppose he could beat McKinley?" she asked with a mischievous grin.

Bill never answered.

* * *

"Charlie, did I tell someone about the young man with the broken ankle?" Bertha asked as they cuddled in bed that night.

"You told me, and I told Bill. He said he'd be takin' care of it."

"You're my hero, ol' man; I don't know what I'd do without you."

"I'm purty pleased with you, too, sweetheart. You and the black done good. Besides winnin' the purse of $1875, I placed bets on you and won us another $1000. And with the black's looks and his racin' reputation, he'll be makin' us a pile of money as a breedin' stallion. . . signed up six mares after the race whist ya was restin'," he said proudly.

"Maybe we can name our expanding homestead, Washakie Ranch," she said. "Whaddya think?"

"That's a fine name, dear," he responded as he snuggled closer.

A FAMILY FOR WASHAKIE RANCH

James McClellan had taken his last name from the only important person he had ever heard of, George McClellan. All of New York City's inhabitants, even street people, knew the mayor's name. The name made him feel significant among the other street kids, gave him pride, hope.

He had dirty blond hair and soulful gray-green eyes, too old for his 11 years. He was small for his age, but wily, strong and resourceful. He'd had to be in order to keep him and his sister, Jane, alive since hitting the streets nigh onto a year before ending up at the Children's Aid Society. James had somewhat enjoyed his time on the street—his freedom, no rules, only those of survival for food and cover. He was quick and stealthy when stealing from the marketplace and lucky not to have been caught. There were no beatings with a strap, wire or stick by a drunken parent or having to endure scalding, abusive remarks like "I hate you" or "I wish you'd never been born." These had been especially hard to hear when directed toward little Janie.

Jane was six years old, blue-eyed and towheaded. Although she was cute as a button, she did not speak. Perpetual cold and hunger kept her silent: no smiles, no laughter. She remembered nothing but hard times.

No, life on the street had been hard, but it had been better than the cruel treatment they had contended with daily at their rent before being abandoned and thrown out by the angry landlord.

In 1854, the Children's Aid Society in New York City initiated a program that placed orphans, foundlings, waifs and street urchins on trains (known as Orphan Trains) going to farming communities in the Midwest and West to be placed in foster homes. This placement was an attempt to provide wholesome homes for those who might otherwise face a life of poverty and crime. Some became foster children or were adopted. Others lived as boarders, apprentices or live-in laborers. Some found good homes; others found a new life of indentured servitude or abuse. Still others ran away or moved on to another family. Billy the Kid came west on an Orphan Train, as did the future governors of South Dakota and Alaska.

The Society had found James and Jane just after the Christmas holiday huddled in their favorite habitat—a basement of a condemned building—with four other homeless street kids varying in age from seven to twelve. They had been immediately seized and taken to the orphanage. They were fed and sheltered, but they had also been forced to stay behind locked doors—free will: gone.

Living at the Society's orphanage for three long months, they had felt like prisoners. James had made few friends besides the four other kids that he'd previously hung with on the streets. Silent Jane made no friends, sticking to her brother like glue and looking to him as her only true guardian.

It wasn't until the night before their departure west that the headmaster told the children they were going on a train to find foster homes. They had bathed, received clean clothes, and their hair tended to.

* * *

Harper's New Monthly Magazine August 1873, praised the "placing-out system" of the Children's Aid Society in New York as "an ingenious effort for the benefit of the destitute children of the city."

At Grand Central Station, placing agents of the Society had herded 45 children into two cars of the Union Pacific Railroad. No amenities, just benches, blankets and windows in which to peer out in wonderment. James had felt a brief sadness at the time of departing from his city, but maybe life would now get better for his sister. He wasn't worried about himself; he could survive. . . he already had.

They had been on various trains for ten days headed toward who-knows-where, eating beans and sage hens caught in the prairie daily by workers. All James knew for sure was they traveled west, forever west, in search of foster families. Already, nine were left in Wisconsin, seventeen in Iowa, including three of his street friends, and fourteen in Nebraska. The Society's agents tried to find families that would keep siblings together so James and Jane were not as "adoptable" as single children. James had never had any formal schooling but had learned to print his name, tally money, and count up to ten. Besides Jane and himself, he figured three children remained, including his street friend Ben.

The conductor had said they would be coming into Casper, Wyoming, the next day—James's anxiety surfaced when he had scolded Jane for knocking his elbow and making him spill some of his beans, which he promptly scooped off the floorboards into his mouth. *What lay ahead next?* He wondered with trepidation. The wheels continued to wail "clickety-clack, clickety-clack" down the track toward their destiny.

Agents, who accompanied the children, placed advance notices of "Homes Wanted for Orphans" in key newspapers of each town in which the Orphan Train would stop. Usually, a local town committee had been at work prior to the arrival of the train, trying to line up good potential families for the expected children.

At Casper, the children paraded into a

meeting hall for inspection. One man, whose family had succumbed to the fever, took in an eight-year-old boy. A farmer came up to James poking and prodding, felt his muscles and commented, "Oh, you'd make a fine working hand on my farm." He showed no interest in Jane.

When he began leading James out of the station, James kicked him, yelling "You either take me an' my sister together or you leave me here."

The children had been specifically told to be on their best behavior and coached to beg for adoption.

The placing agent considered James's performance incorrigible. He promptly ushered brother and sister into a back room with a severe reprimand, "James, you better cooperate and show some manners or you and your sister will be left out here in the west without a home. It might not be possible to place both you and Jane in the same home, but separate homes for now will be better than no homes. Do you understand?"

"Yes, sir," James replied. "But I don't like it none," he hissed through his teeth. Tears silently spilled down Jane's cheeks as she clung to James's arm.

A 12-year-old boy went with the farmer who had wanted James. Three children,

Ben, James and Jane, and one placing agent boarded the train again heading west to the next stop, Lander.

James awoke that morning to rain and wind lashing the roof and sides of the train. Thunder rumbled above the noise of the wheels, and lightening flashed, brightening the graying dawn inside the car. Jane hid her head deep beneath her blanket. James had just settled back for a nap when the train began to slow. As the big wheels shrieked, grinding on the iron rails, the train came to a shuddering stop.

As the three children disembarked at Lander in the blowing rain, a town committee member rushed them into the station house for the usual public scrutiny. Whereas the weather was foul, only a few of community members were on hand. A husband and wife showed much interest in—Jane.

"She's beautiful but rather shy," the woman said to her husband. "I think I'd really like to have her. What do you think?"

"How old are you girl?" the man demanded. "Speak up."

"She's 'bout six and she's my sister," James answered. "She used to talk but ain't spoke for a while now." He did not tell them it had been two years of silence following physical pain, mental abuse, hunger and cold. "She'll be alright if you takes me too," he added.

"We already have five boys and don't need 'nother one. Wife needs a girl to help cook 'n take care of the younguns.

"This one'll do," he said to the placing agent.

James was distraught but tried not to show it for Jane's sake. She wept silently, tears flooding her eyes and rolling down her pallid cheeks. He took her aside and whispered, "You must be brave, Janie. I'll come back for you soon's I can. First, I have to go to Cody and hope to get adopted. Then I'll have to get us a horse and learn the lay of the land so we can make it on our own. But I promise I'll be back. 'Til then, you stay with this family; they'll take care of you."

With that said, he gave her a big hug and turned to leave quickly so he couldn't see the pain and fright in her eyes.

The remaining two children, their placing agent John, and a pinstripe-suited drummer hugging his sample case of wares boarded a stagecoach going north through Wind River Canyon to catch the Bridger Trail—last stop, Cody, Wyoming.

The rain ceased but left behind myriad mud holes deep enough that one wheel soon became mired almost to the axle. The stagecoach driver, in a dour mood, unharnessed one horse and rode it to town and then brought back a second span of harnessed horses along with another employee, called a "tender". A tender fed, watered, cared for, harnessed and unharnessed the horses and helped wherever needed, as it was beneath most drivers, known as "whips", to do anything except drive. Apparently, Hap, the driver, considered himself one of these elite. Once harnessed, the team of four hauled the stage with much less difficulty over the deeply rutted trail.

James, morose but curious and trying not to think about Jane, watched out the windows expecting, hoping, to see Indians or robbers around every bend. . . he'd listened to and believed too many tales related as facts by the older kids during the boring ride across the country. As their train had chased the North Platte the length of Nebraska, James had wished for an exciting deviation like train robbers—but then, who would want a bunch of kids he had concluded. On the other hand, Indians liked to take kids and bring them up as their own—or so he'd heard. No one told him that, presently, most Indians lived on reservations, like Chief Washakie's friendly Shoshone tribe on the Wind River Reservation, which they were traveling through.

James talked little the first day, taking in the vistas of contrasting red rock and blue sky and the Wind River meandering between canyon walls. They traveled 15 to 20 miles before the coach stopped at a station allowing just enough time to eat, catch a few winks of sleep and change teams. The horses fascinated James as he'd never been around any in the city. He questioned both Hap and Cliff, the tender, about the horses' names, who they belonged to, how old, what kind, what they ate, and on and on. He began assisting Cliff when the horses needed attention. Whenever the stage stopped for a rest, he helped Cliff unharness and lead them to water.

"Suppose I could ride one sometime?" he asked.

"Nah, don't have time to fool with them nags. They need to rest in between working, and so do I," Cliff replied. "And I'm going to do that right now," he said as he headed for a pile of loose hay and lay down on his slicker. James stayed with the horses while they ate, grooming and talking to them as if they were his best friends. He felt a real rapport with the horses and wished he were old enough to be hired on as a tender. He kept it in mind for the future. . . *maybe someday*, he thought.

At a junction in the Bridger Trail, Ben and James explored a bit, subsequent to his tending the horses. After all, they were in the middle of nowhere with no place to go and were not about to run away. They sat on a ledge overhanging the way station.

"You know, James, even when we both get adopted, we can still be friends. John says there are folks waiting in Cody for each of us so we'll be near each other."

"Yeah, I've known you most of a year now; you're like a brother to me. I sure do miss my sister, though. Ain't right us not being together. Hope she's alright."

"I heard you saying you'd come for her. If you do and need help or a friend to travel with, hope you look me up," Ben said in earnest. "I'll go with you if I can get away."

"*I'll* get away; I know that. . . have to keep my promise. Thanks for your offer; I might take you up on it when the time comes."

* * *

Bertha Daye, younger wife and partner of former mountain man turned rancher Charlie Daye, made the trip to Cody for supplies by herself this month in their newly purchased buckboard. Expanding business at Washakie Ranch kept them both very busy: Bertha with horse breeding, training and selling, Charlie with building additional sheds, repairing fences and mending tack. Both catered to guests that booked weeklong stays at their ranch, riding trails or packing into the Shoshone National Forest.

Just so happened a notice reading:

WANTED
Homes for Orphan Children
Meet at The Irma   May 12

was posted at the Irma Hotel's bar. This was Bertha's favorite watering hole where she stopped for a drink and food every time she was in town. *Hmmmm,* she said to herself. *I wonder...*

"Hey, Dave," Bertha called to the bartender. "What do you know about this?" She waved the notice in his face.

"Not much more than what it says: orphan children were put on a train from New York City and shipped west to find homes, supposed to be here day after tomorrow, coming from Lander on the stage."

She headed for the door with the notice in hand.

"Gotta leave that notice here, Bertha," yelled Dave. "Some other people might be interested in one of them children."

She jammed it back on the nail and hurried

out—no drink, no food. "I'll be damned," exclaimed Dave.

Bertha went straight to the general store for the necessary grain and food supplies. Soon, with the buckboard loaded, she hustled Charlie's mules, unhappy to be in harness, out of town, hurrying back to their ranch on the North Fork of the Shoshone.

That evening as Bertha nestled in bed next to her husband, she whispered, "Charlie, ever think of having kids?"

"No, but I don't mind tryin' to make some anytime ya want." He cuddled closer wrapping one arm and leg around her.

"Get off me, Charlie. I'm serious." She sat upright.

"So am I," *now*, he thought to himself as he also sat up in bed. Charlie being in his late forties added, "I figure I'm too old to do the baby thing, and honey, I didn't know you wanted any."

"I'd been too busy to think much about it."

"That's the point. Ain't we busy 'nough without babies?"

"I don't mean that kind of kids."

"What other kind are there?" Charlie asked, mystified as well as worried where this might be leading.

"Well, let me tell you what I've been thinking on since I went into Cody today. I saw a notice that there is a stage coming into town day after tomorrow bringing orphan kids, at least half grown, that came from the East on a train to find homes, and Charlie, we have a home, plenty of room to spare, and you have so much you could teach a kid, especially a boy, and he could help you too," she rambled on without taking a breath.

"Well dear, I guess we could try it if'n you're sure ya want to do the mother thing; I could try being a father. . .might be nice to pass on what my pa taught me as well as what I've learnt in life."

"But what if it don't work out? What if he hates us? What do we do then?" he added.

"I can't imagine a boy from the East not loving this land, horses, and especially you, Charlie. Let's go into town and see," she said as she snuggled back down next to him.

"Yes, dear."

* * *

Two days later the stage rolled into Cody, stopping at the Irma to pick up returning passengers and change horses. Bertha and Charlie waited in anticipation. There were two other people waiting, a couple that Charlie knew lived a ways down on the South Fork, named Weston. They nodded and smiled in acknowledgment.

James and Ben looked forward to their final stage stop. As much as James enjoyed tending horses and observing the variety of western scenery, the stagecoach benches were hard. His butt was sore, and he needed a bath. The prairie dust covered him from top to toe, and his eyes peered through a mask of dust as he stepped out of the coach, looking at a handful of people looking back at him.

John said, "Let's get you boys inside and washed up a bit before you meet your new families," as he ushered them into the hotel. After a cursory washing, John presented the boys to the waiting couples. Immediately, blond-haired Bertha was drawn to James's fair skin, dirty-blond hair and small build. The Westons were as attracted toward the taller and dark-haired Ben. Bertha nudged Charlie, urging him to follow her lead as she approached James.

"Hi, I'm Bertha Daye and this is my husband, Charlie," she said as they shook hands, noting his young but firm grip. "What's *your* name, young man?"

"I'm James McClellan," he replied with pride. She liked that.

"And, how old are ya, James McClellan?" Charlie inquired with a hint of western twang and a twinkle in his eye that James liked.

"I'm 11, sir."

Seeing his discomfort at being interviewed amongst observers, Bertha suggested, "Would you like to eat with us here at the hotel? We left our ranch at sunup this morning and are mighty hungry 'bout now."

"Yes, ma'am."

"Please call us Bertha and Charlie." She smiled to ease the tension.

"Yes, ma'am. I mean Bertha, ma'am."

She laughed and led the way into the Irma's dining room. The Westons, Ben, and John followed suit.

They conversed lightly in between bites, noting that James ate with gusto and answered questions with one word answers, not volunteering information. However, when Bertha mentioned raising horses, his eyes shone with interest. She felt—hoped—that his reticence was only a temporary state. She figured: *If I found myself transported east to New York City, guess I'd be a bit skittish too.*

Charlie identified with James's shy manner and liked the boy, straight away. He and Bertha decided with a nod between them that they wanted to take James home with them.

"James, would you like to come to our ranch and live with us?" Bertha asked.

"That would be right fine with me. Would I get to help with the horses?" he asked with enthusiasm.

"I 'spect so as that's mostly what we do at the ranch," Charlie chuckled.

"First, I'd like to say 'bye to my friend Ben over there with them other people."

"Sure, we'll speak with your guardian, John, then meet you right outside with our mules and buckboard."

"*Mules?*" They heard him exclaim as he sprinted off.

The three left Cody with James seated between Bertha and Charlie. They pointed out the other two high points of interest to James: the cattle pens and rodeo grounds, and the Shoshone Dam project—the first point of interest being the Irma Hotel, known as "The best hotel in the West" as Buffalo Bill Cody often bragged. Following the North Fork of the Shoshone, they bounced along in the buckboard, explaining how they had met, the pack trips they guided and the highlights of their horse business. As Bertha explained, the business began with catching the wild mustang, Washaki, and her racing him in

Cody's Fourth of July Race a few years back, winning the purse money that financed their breeding ranch.

James was enthralled. "I learned how to take care of horses helping the stagecoach tender, but I don't know nothing about mules. Do you handle them like horses?" he asked.

Charlie's favorite animals were his mules; he responded, "Mules are smarter 'n horses, more surefooted on mountain trails and eat less; otherwise you handle 'em 'bout the same.

"Want to take these lines and drive 'em a ways?" He handed the reins to a smiling James.

"The mule on the left is Dot, and the other is Dan. Shake the reins a little and say 'Giddyap' to get 'em going, and pull back sayin' 'whoa' when ya want to stop. Just keep 'em followin' this road. I'll be right here beside ya if'n ya needs help."

Bertha was pleased. *Things are going just fine,* she thought.

And things did go well. James began helping Bertha feed, groom and water the horses. He learned to saddle and bridle a horse and harness the mules. She gave him a small, aging brood mare, named Brit, whom he fell off, repeatedly, until finally he learned to keep his balance on her back and guide her at the same time. He rode with Charlie or their foreman, Larry, when they went out checking fences or whenever he could find an excuse to ride. Bertha and Charlie adored him, and although they didn't learn much about his past, they didn't press him, figuring if his past was important, it would come out eventually—when he was ready to tell them.

However, he did talk and talk and talk about horses, ranching and riding and asked question upon question. Every day was a learning experience for him, and he loved it. Mid-summer, he helped Charlie pack the mules and worked his first guest pack trip into the Shoshone National Forest for five days. He learned fast and was responsible and polite to the guests, although still shy.

James admitted that he had never been to school, so in late summer, Bertha enrolled him in the Wapiti Valley School, a few miles west of their ranch. His daily routine from then on was to help her do morning chores and then attend school for a half day, meeting up with Charlie after lunch to assist him in doing whatever he had planned to do for the afternoon.

Life could not have been better for him, except—what about his promise to his sister? Not knowing how they would react, he wasn't sure he dared tell Bertha and Charlie; trusting was still foreign to him. However, before winter he figured he'd have to go get Jane, bring her back with him and hope they would accept her too. If not, he would work to pay for his horse, and then he and Jane would be on their own again, only this time in the West.

September arrived, bringing cooler weather and golden hues of aspens, exhibiting their brilliance between the green of conifer trees—it was time to find Jane. James's usual sunny self became sullen and quiet. He maintained his daily routine but without smiles or conversation. Bertha and Charlie were both mystified by his change in behavior but did not ask questions; they had no experience raising a child.

James was deep in thought most of the time, arguing with himself the rest of the time: *Should I tell them about Jane? Should I ask their help? Should I tell them I am going?* No, no, no, were his answers based on past dealings with adults. *They will not understand and will either forbid me to go or tell me to go permanently and find another home.* Neither result was what he wanted; yet, he felt he *must* get to his sister and try to bring her back to the ranch—soon.

Therefore, he planned to leave by himself, riding one horse and leading a pack mule to carry provisions. He wished he could take the mustang, Washakie, knowing that he was a racer and could make fast time. But, even though he had befriended the stallion, he had not been allowed to ride him, as Bertha said that he was a one-woman horse. So he settled for his mare, Brit.

He schemed what he would need to take and where to store it until the time was right and he could get away without being caught. The first of October, by the light of a full moon, he quietly saddled Brit, packed Dan, the mule, and left a printed note nailed to the barn door. He was riding out of Cody before Bertha and Charlie knew he was gone.

"Bertha," Charlie shouted as he burst through the kitchen door. "James's gone. Look."

He handed her the note.

> must fine sistr
>
> James

"What in damnation does that mean? What sister? Where?"

"Dear, I don't know any more 'n you. Only that he took ol' Brit, and Dan's gone too."

"That little devil must have been planning this for some time, and that's why he's been so gloomy. Wonder why he didn't tell us?"

"Don't know dear, but then, we don't know much about him or what he's suffered afore he came to us," Charlie replied. "Guess we shoulda asked," he added.

"Well we can't just let him go, Charlie; I love the little cuss and besides, Brit won't make it two days riding before she'll lame up. Can you track him and see which way he rode while I saddle us a couple of horses?"

By the time Charlie returned from the gate, Bertha had filled their canteens, stuffed some food into saddlebags, tied a slicker and blanket onto each saddle and had just finished tacking up Washakie and another mustang, Greystone. She reckoned they'd need stamina and endurance on this trip—mustangs, long on both attributes, were her best choice.

"Looks like the boy headed east toward Cody."

"Then let's go talk to Ben at the Westons' and see if he can shed some light on James's *sister* and where he'd go looking for her."

Leaving Larry to take care of the ranch, Bertha and Charlie rode off at a fast gallop toward Cody.

Amos and Mary Weston lived a mile down the South Fork Trail, before coming in to Cody.

They had three small daughters, one son and now Ben had joined them. They had just finished breakfast when Bertha and Charlie raced up.

Amos Weston greeted them at the porch, "Howdy Bertha, Charlie. Ben, Adam, take care of them horses, curry 'em down, give 'em some water and feed," he ordered his boys.

"Come on in, folks. Would you like some coffee? Or the Missus can whip up some hotcakes?"

"Coffee's fine, thanks," Bertha said.

"Looks like you been ridin' hard. Y'all having some trouble over your way?" Amos asked with concern.

"Things been going pretty well 'til this morning when our foster boy James ran off, leaving a note saying something about finding his sister. We don't know what it means or where he's gone. We're right worried. We'd like to speak to Ben and see if he can tell us anything that makes sense."

"Ben, come on in here, please," Mary Weston called.

He came on the run, "Yes, ma'am."

"You remember the family James went with, Mr. and Mrs. Daye, they want to ask you a few questions."

"Hi, Ben," Bertha said. "We like James real well, and we've been getting along just fine. Then this morning we found a note that said he's gone to find his sister! We don't know about any sister, do you?"

"Yes, ma'am. I know he has one, got left off down in Lander. Name's Jane. They's real close; she not talking and being so little and all, so he promised he'd come for her soon's he could. I offered to help him back before I got me a home. 'Spect he knows I wouldn't go with him now, and I ain't seen him since we parted."

"Well I'll be doggoned," Charlie exclaimed. "Sure wishin' he'd a told us 'stead of takin' off by hisself."

"Thanks, Ben," Bertha said. "You've been a big help. And thanks for the coffee, Mary. We best be going now. I'm guessing James is still another three to four hours ride ahead of us."

"Ben, you and your brother go to fetch Mr. and Mrs. Daye's horses. Do you need me to ride with you?" asked Amos.

"No, but thanks for the offer. 'Spect we can catch him afore sunset if'n we hurry," Charlie replied as he and Bertha mounted up.

Now that they knew the direction the boy was heading, they took a shortcut skirting Cody, saving them several miles riding.

* * *

James had made good time following the road into Cody; he'd trotted most of the way. However, the mare had slowed to a walk for the past few miles and refused to go any faster. He felt her walking with a limp so he dismounted and checked her feet for stones or bruises as he'd seen Charlie do. Nothing wrong. Tying Dan's lead rope to his saddle horn, he decided to walk for a while to give Brit a rest.

After a few miles he came to a creek where he watered the animals, dropped their ropes so they could graze and then quenched his own thirst before digging a cold piece of venison out of his pack. He gulped it down in a hurry, as he'd skipped breakfast. He settled down to rest a short spell.

As the sun began to lose itself behind the horizon, he heard voices coming down the trail. He gathered the nearby grazing animals and led them down the creek, meaning to hide among the cottonwoods, but Brit whinnied revealing their whereabouts.

"Hey, looky here Cy," the taller of the two said. "That boy's got hisself a horse and a packed mule.

"Boy, we're needin' some provisions; come back here so's we can make a deal," he hollered.

James had been on the streets long enough to know not to mix with strangers if he could help it. He'd meant to hightail it out of there pronto, but the two riders were upon him before he could mount the uneasy mare. The mule spooked free of his grasp.

He punched, kicked and bit as they wrestled him to the ground.

"Now kid, you can do this the hard way and get yo'self hurt, or relax and we'll leave a coupla coins for them animals and grub." He winked at his partner.

"You can't take them 'cause they ain't mine," James protested as they began tying him to a tree.

"So whaddya do, steal 'em?" Cy chuckled.

"No; they belong to my ma and pa. They're meeting me on the trail up from Lander any time now." He lied.

"Well, now, who's your parents? Maybe we'll just wait for them and stock up on a few more provisions." Tall man laughed.

"Bertha and Charlie Daye are my parents," James announced proudly.

"Bertha. Bertha Daye? I'll be damned. I'd rather wrestle a grizzly sow with cubs than have that woman find we tied up her youngun. I heard tell 'bout her temper, and I ain't stickin' around. Let's round up them critters and get outta here."

Suddenly a man's voice called from the darkening trail, "Hello, comin' in."

"That you, James?" a female added.

"Forget them animals. Let's ride," tall man said as he mounted and sped in the opposite direction of the voices. Cy followed at once.

"Over here," James cried out.

"What in tarnation happened to you?" Bertha asked as she untied James and hugged him.

"Two men just left, tied me up and was gonna take Brit and Dan, but they heard you coming and got scared," James declared.

Charlie gave chase until he knew for sure the two were long gone and then returned to see to James and the horses. Bertha started a fire to settle in for the night. As the three sat together around the fire, Bertha said, "Okay, James, time to tell us about your sister, and *everything.*"

He did. . . his whole story: the beatings, the name calling, being abandoned, near to starvation, his sister's silence, the Society orphanage, his friendship with Ben, and the train and stagecoach rides.

"You had us frightened and confused, James. Why didn't you tell us you wanted to find your sister? Or ask our help? We thought you liked being part of our family."

"I love you and Charlie. I didn't ask you to help or tell you I was going because I was afraid you'd say I couldn't. And I *promised*. . ." Overcome with fatigue and relief, he collapsed onto Bertha's lap. She held him cradled in her arms while Charlie made bedrolls from the blankets and slickers they'd brought. He laid James gently onto his and turned to Bertha. "Guess we need to see 'bout this little girl—right dear," he said reading her mind.

"So what now?" Bertha asked as she lay next to Charlie. Ever the practical one, he said, "Lets sleep on it an' the three of us talk in the mornin'."

Daybreak found them anxious for decisions. Charlie spoke first. "James, I know ya want to find your sister, so Bertha and I will do what we can to help ya."

"But," Bertha added, "you need to be thinking, James, that she might be very happy right where she is. . . and if so, are you willing to leave her there and come back with us?"

"Yes, ma'am. . . Bertha. I just need to 'fill my promise and make sure she's happy. My home's with you and Charlie."

"Well then, looks like we could be gone for 'nother nine days," Charlie said. "Larry can take care of the ranch 'n horses, but we need more provisions and 'nother horse. Brit's too old to make the trip, along with bein' six months with foal." James's eyes bugged out and a smile spread across his otherwise pensive face.

"I was thinkin', an old-time trapper friend of mine named Smitty lives near here, and we might stop to see if'n he has a spare horse we could borrow and leave Brit to rest up. I figure we can get supplies at the Meeteese Mercantile."

"I love you, ol' man," Bertha said as she kissed him on the check. "You always come through with a plan."

Bertha reached down taking James's hand and swinging him up behind her saddle as Washakie rolled his eyes but didn't object. Charlie led Dan; Brit followed at her own speed.

Three days later they rode into Riverton. Charlie inquired from the bartender at the Ol' Wyoming Saloon if he'd heard about a family that had adopted a girl-child from the Orphan Train about five to six months past. No success. "But, the shot of whiskey tasted mighty fine," he confessed upon meeting back up with Bertha.

She said, "I got some information from the general store owner. Says he knows a family named Johnston, about halfway here to Lander, on the Sage Creek River, that had talked of getting a girl from some adoption place back east. Might be them."

Encouraged, they followed the storeowner's directions to a small cabin with chickens scratching in the dusty front yard and what looked like hog pens in back.

As they rode up, Charlie yelled, "Hello, the house."

A woman came out holding a baby, with another child toddling alongside grabbing her dress for support. James recognized her at once and started to dismount. Bertha said, "Wait. We need to be invited first.

"We're Bertha and Charlie Daye. Are you the folks that adopted a girl from the Orphan Train in Lander?"

"So what if we are? What do you want with us?" a man asked as he approached from behind the cabin.

"We'd like to talk, and the little girl's brother, James, is with us and he'd like to visit with his sister—if that's alright with you."

"Don't matter; the girl's dumb, don't talk and is so quiet she's spooky. Wife don't get much work out of her. . . weak, always crying. Not worth the cost to feed her.

"Jane, get out here," Mr. Johnston hollered.

A little blonde-headed girl, wearing boys' trousers peered around the cabin door. When she spotted James, she flew down the steps into his arms, sobbing and laughing at the same time.

Giving the two some time to themselves, the Dayes asked Mr. Johnston if they could water their animals.

"Charlie, my heart's breaking for that poor little girl. Did you see the bruises on her arms? What do we do now? Can't let her stay where she's abused and not wanted."

"I'll try a little negotiatin', dear. I've met his type afore at tradin' posts. . . always lookin' for a deal."

When they returned from the creek, Charlie, a mountain man of few words, spoke softly to the Johnstons. "As the girl ain't working out well with your family, we could take her off'n your hands. We don't have no other kids 'sides James."

"Well, I ain't just giving her to you. I fed that girl all these months, and she never earned her keep."

"What if I gave ya all the food we have on that there mule?"

"I dunno; we could sure use the mule too."

"Nope. No mule. We've got some blankets I'll throw in, that's it. . . whaddya say, deal?"

"Suppose so," Johnston grumbled.

"Wife, the brat's going with these folks. Take the food and blankets off'n that mule, give 'em the girl's dress, hat and coat she brought with her and don't let 'em take them trousers." He stomped off heading to the hog pens with nary another word.

On the return trip north, Bertha tried to convince Jane to ride with her on Washakie. However, Jane clung to her brother so fiercely that Bertha relented when he said, "Janie ain't used to you yet. She can ride behind me. My saddle is big enough for both of us. I'll be right careful.

"Now you hold on to me real tight, Jane," he told her, like the caring older brother he'd always been. She wrapped her little arms around his waist and smiled.

A picture of contentment, thought Bertha with compassion.

On the way back through Riverton, they stopped at the general store, bought a pair of trousers and three blankets.

Around the campfire that evening, after the kids were tucked into their bedrolls, Bertha said, "You did good back there, ol' man. How'd you know Mr. Johnston would let the girl go?"

"Makin' my livin' dickerin' in the tradin' business all them years learnt me to read people purty good. I could tell he was a greedy no-account. All Jane was to him was a slave, so I bartered as I used to do with my pelts."

"I'm glad you're my husband," she replied giving his hand a squeeze and leading him to their blanket.

In the morning, Jane trudged along with her brother helping as best she could, doing whatever he did. He told her the horses' names and showed her how to brush *with* the hair not against it. "And you be real nice to your new ma, Bertha, and our pa, Charlie. They've been right good to me, and they'll treat *you* good too. They won't ever leave us or beat us; they'll just love us, if'n you let 'em." Jane stopped brushing Washakie a moment and laid her cheek against his soft shoulder.

When it came time to mount up, Jane turned to Bertha and spoke: "Can I ride 'Washy' with you today, Ma?"

TRIALS AND TRIBULATIONS OF PARENTHOOD

When Bertha had become Charlie's wife and partner, they had expanded his one-room bachelor cabin by adding a bedroom, front porch and an outhouse. Over the years, a six-stall horse barn replaced his former mule lean-to, and two paddocks were built to separate the breeding mares, or recently weaned foals, from the herd or to hold pack animals overnight instead of being turned loose in the hundred-acre pasture.

When their family had expanded with the addition of James, an eleven-year-old, and his six-year-old sister, Jane, they had expanded the cabin again. They built a loft for James's bedroom and added another smaller room for Jane. The porch, now covered, surrounded the cabin on three sides; the outhouse was moved nearer the cabin.

Jane loved and felt comfortable with the smaller animals; the horses—except "Washy", her name for Bertha's stallion, Washakie—intimidated her. Charlie and James built a henhouse for Jane's chicks and chickens. It was her responsibility to feed, water and gather eggs each day. A month ago they'd acquired two puppies: a black male James called Bear and a spotted female that Jane laid claim to and named Pepper. After two years of silence, she now talked nonstop to whomever or whatever would listen: people, mules, horses, chickens, or puppies. Bertha enrolled her in school two weeks after she joined the Daye family, and with James, attended every weekday morning. She had never been happier.

Having the same uncanny rapport with horses as Bertha, James was already an avid horseman. He caught on quickly to helping her train the foals and yearlings. After returning from Lander with Jane, they'd retired his aging brood mare, Brit, and he'd been given a green-broke three-year-old chestnut gelding named Chester. It was not unusual for him to ride off by himself for hours at a time—that is, when he was not in school or helping at the ranch. Bertha and Charlie were at first concerned about his solitary riding habits; however, they knew his experience as a youth on the streets of

New York City had taught him self-confidence and responsibility, so they let him have his time alone with his horse. Charlie, living as a mountain man and bachelor for some 30 years before meeting Bertha, understood his son's love of the forest with its tranquility and quiet solitude.

Come May, Charlie was restless, and after talking it over with Bertha, he decided to take James on a long weekend pack trip, checking trails up Green Creek to Table Mountain. Guests would be coming in June and he needed the trails cleared and campsites ready.

"Hey, James. How'd you like to help pack up to Table Mountain with me this weekend? Be leavin' Friday noon after school. We'd camp two nights an' be back late Sunday. Whaddya say?" Charlie asked nonchalantly, knowing what the answer would be.

"Wow, I sure would! Been looking forward to summer guest pack trips. But it would be great to go with just us two, Pa. Can I ride Chester?"

"I 'spect so; be good trainin' for him. Still pretty cold up there on that mountain this time o' year, so's we needin' bedrolls, an' be sure to take a warm coat, hat, boots an' an extra pair of gloves. We might even pack an extra blanket or two, just in case," he added.

"What about me and Ma?" Janie inquired, pouting a little. "What will we do while you're gone?" She hadn't been without her brother since they'd found her and brought her to their ranch last October.

"Well, I guess we could drive to Cody and pick up some supplies for the ranch and maybe a summer dress and shoes for you. You sure are growing fast, girl."

"Can I get a candy, too, Ma?" she asked, hopefully.

Bertha, still getting used to being called *Ma*, replied, "Yes, you can swap one of your fresh eggs for *one* of Mr. Beasley's rock candies. And don't you try to talk him into two, like you did last time." She chuckled and winked at Charlie and James.

James smiled. He was glad to see his sister so happy with their new family and surroundings. Being abused and then abandoned, she'd had a tough first six years of her life. . . he figured she deserved to be coddled and a little spoiled.

Friday afternoon found Charlie riding his big bay gelding, Rooster—who was the hefty size of a draft horse—leading Dan the mule packed with axes, saws and shovels to clear trails and clean out fire pits; a tarp covered blankets and foodstuff. James, all bundled up thanks to Bertha, followed with Chester who pranced and danced impatient to be under way. . . he'd soon get his fill of exercise.

After the "men" were on their way, Bertha set about catching Dot and Digger. Mules can have an ornery disposition and seems neither mule was anxious to leave the herd. She had to rope and lead each separately to the corral. Dot came along once her halter was on, but Digger resisted to the point of balking with all four feet planted as Bertha tried to convince him to enter the corral gate.

Bertha's forte was horses not mules. Charlie handled the mules. Frustration got the better of her.

"You no-good #@%&* polecat. Get your sorry #@% in here before I put a stick to you," she threatened.

"What's a polecat, Ma? Are you cussing?"

Bertha had forgotten little ears listening and eyes watching her display of temper. Taking a deep breath, she apologized, "Yes, I'm cussing, and I'm sorry you heard that. I'll try to use better words, but these mules make me so angry. . . give me one horse to a dozen mules any day."

"Maybe you can tell Digger we'll give him some grain if he comes into the corral," Jane suggested as she rattled the grain pan. At that,

Digger pushed Bertha aside in his hurry to get inside.

"*Mules,*" Bertha muttered.

Almost ready to leave for Cody, Jane asked, "Can we take Pepper with us, Ma?" Not wanting to be separated from her new puppy she pleaded, "Can we, please?"

"No, she needs to be with her brother."

Bertha would soon regret not giving a fuller explanation or answer.

"Now take this nest of eggs, carefully, and wrap them in the blanket in the buckboard, and I'll be right out."

On the way into Cody Bertha noticed the sky becoming crowded with graying clouds. She was briefly concerned about her men as there was always the chance of a late spring snowstorm in the mountains. However, she trusted her husband and knew he'd look after James—so do not worry, she reminded herself.

Approaching the Shoshone Dam just outside Cody, the sun burst forth its golden rays and the sky turned azure blue, which served to allay any lingering unease she might have about bad weather. The dam construction began two years prior and when finished would form a much-needed reservoir to be used for irrigation by local farmers and ranchers.

Some called it a potential "God-send," however their friend Buffalo Bill Cody was more than a little instrumental in coordinating the project between the Wyoming Board of Land Commissioners and the federal government.

After a few miles on the trail, Jane curled up in a blanket and lay down in the back to nap. Now tying up at the rail in front of the general store, Bertha spoke to her, "Janie, wake up. We're in Cody. Do you want to come into Beasley's with me?"

"I'll be right in, Ma," she answered with a yawn and a full stretch.

Bertha proceeded into the store expecting Jane to follow.

What happened next was still a little vague, even after Jane later filled in the details. According to her, she had put BOTH puppies under the buckboard blankets back at the ranch. . . *so they would be together*, she explained afterward. When she'd climbed down, she thought the puppies were asleep and would stay where they were—wrong—they both plummeted off the tailgate into the street, attempting to follow. Bear made it under the wooden sidewalk; Pepper got her paw stomped on by a horse trotting by.

Mayhem ensued.

Pepper yelped. Jane screamed. Then she ran to fetch her hurt puppy, bumping into the front wheel of a buggy and tumbling head over heels backward, landing under Dot's belly. The horse pulling the buggy whinnied in fright as its driver drew on the reins to keep it from bolting. The mules brayed in disgust.

Hearing her daughter scream, Bertha rushed out just in time to see the wheel knock Jane to the ground. Her protective instinct came to the forefront as she scooped both child and puppy into her arms and began cussing out the buggy driver for his negligence.

"Ma'am, she ran into me. And besides, why weren't you watching out for the little brat and her #@$& pups? What kinda mother are you, anyway? Coulda gotten herself run over, rushing into a busy street like that."

Enough said in front of the child, Bertha thought guiltily as she turned and stepped onto the walkway still hugging Jane and Pepper and stooping to pick up Bear. Sheridan Avenue, the main street in Cody, *was* incredibly busy these days compared to years ago when she'd married Charlie at the preacher's parsonage of Cody's Trinity Lutheran. With the completion of the Burlington Railroad branch and the Cody Road to Yellowstone, the street was fraught with miners, cattlemen, ranchers, merchants, drummers, townsfolk and tourists. *I should* have taken her hand and kept her with me. I *am* a bad mother, she chastised herself.

"I love you, Ma," whispered the bleeding, bruised and bumped, but still intact, little girl. "Can I get my candy now?"

"Yes, sweetheart, after I've checked your bruises."

Much to her relief, Bertha learned kids were amazingly resilient. She hoped Charlie fared better with his adventure into the mountains with James than she had in town with Janie. She couldn't wait to have her family all back together again, safe at the ranch.

* * *

May in Wyoming is crisp and, when the sun shines, perfect weather for horseback trekking. Most wild animals had already migrated to higher summer pastures, but some were still grazing the lower ranges. It was through these lower foothills that Charlie and James rode Friday afternoon. They startled mule deer with newborn fawns and watched golden eagles soar above the cliffs. Jackrabbits abounded, and therefore coyotes were prevalent, undaunted by human presence.

"What say we gets ourselves a hare for supper?" Charlie said as one jumped across their trail. "Here, take this rifle an' walk a spell; don't want that youngun of yours spookin' you off his back whilst you're shootin'. You lead, quiet like, up ahead. I'll tie Chester to the mule."

Before long, James spotted a jackrabbit just off the trail and signaled Charlie to hold up. He took aim, caressed the trigger, and fired. The rabbit leaped up into the air and then fell in a heap to the ground.

"How's that, Pa?" James announced proudly.

"Mighty fine, son," Charlie replied. "Mighty fine. Guess all that practice shootin' this past winter paid off. Sure will taste good roasted on a spit tonight, and I'll make us some of my de-licious pan biscuits.

"Talkin' 'bout food's makin' me hungry. Let's move along a little faster, son; we're comin' into some wide-open country for the next few miles," he added as he urged his horse into a slow lope.

Wapiti Valley was greening and pristine—one of the most beautiful places in the civilized world, according to Charlie. Here they began following Green Creek south and upward into the Shoshone National Forest toward Table Mountain. Due to a milder than usual winter, they found the trails in fair condition, so far having to clear away only fallen branches and deadwood. A mile up the creek, they came across a washout where the snowmelt had caused water to overflow the creek's banks, destroying the trail.

"James, this is gonna to take a while. You lead Rooster up the trail a piece and you'll come to a clearin' where we'll camp tonight. Unsaddle the horses, hobble 'em and turn 'em loose to graze; then come back to help me finish up. I'll keep Dan with me."

"Yes, sir." James enjoyed the feeling of trust Charlie instilled when he gave him responsibility. He hoped he could live up to it.

As he followed the trail around a corner, he spotted the clearing up ahead, and there was a moose. James didn't know much about moose—they didn't roam city streets—but he *did* know they grew as large as a horse, and this one wasn't *that* big. *If it's a calf, the mother cow will be around and that might not be good,* he figured. Not knowing exactly what to do or not to do, he noted the horses were relaxed, so he dismounted and tended to them as the young moose watched from the forest edge. James walked back down the trail toward his pa, looking back over his shoulder as he heard the moose's hoofbeats—amble away in the opposite direction. *Whew*, he said to himself.

Later, when James told his pa about the moose, Charlie explained, "Probably a yearlin' or two-year-old run off by his ma 'cause a new calf's been born. They're curious, not very smart and not usually dangerous lessen a cow is protecting her calf, or a bull is in his fall rut—then you sure wanna move fast and stay outta their way."

Charlie liked the prideful feeling of teaching his son the knowledge his father had passed down to him. Real *comfortable feelin', this parentin' business,* he decided as he fell asleep beside his son.

* * *

They awoke to a cold gray morning with low-hanging clouds. After a breakfast of jerky and beans, they packed up and crossed the icy creek to find two downed trees blocking their ascent. They sawed them into large pieces and hauled them to the side and then proceeded up the trail, reinforcing stone steps along the way so heavy rains wouldn't make channels and gullies, washing the trail away. As they continued to climb steep narrow switchbacks, snow began to fall. Soon, it was coming down heavier, causing the horses to slip and lose their footing.

Charlie was concerned about both Chester and James's inexperience handling slippery terrain. He kept looking back to see if they were doing okay. Suddenly, he saw Chester's hind feet slip off the side of a steep portion of the trail, and he yelled, "James, lean forward and urge him upward. That's it. He can make it if'n you help him."

Chester scrambled back up onto the snowy trail. James was doing his best to stay calm, ride balanced, and keep his young horse from sensing any nervousness. Chester needed all the reassurance he could give him right now.

Reaching a plateau near the top, Charlie halted in a shelter of firs to rest their animals and plan what to do next. The storm had now reached blizzard conditions with wind blowing the snow around so fiercely they could barely see in front of them.

"Good boy," James said, patting his horse to keep him steady.

Charlie, trying to sound calmer than he felt, said, "We need to put up for the night; can't go back down in this weather. There's a cleft in the mountainside not far from here, and a cave where we can sit out the storm." *That is, if a bear or wolf hasn't claimed it already,* he thought, but didn't say.

With zero visibility, it would have been a difficult task finding the cave for most men. However, Charlie, born and bred in the mountains, knew this forest like the back of his hand and managed to locate it within a half hour's ride. James held the horses and mule while Charlie climbed up and checked out the cave for signs of unwanted animal life. Finding no live beasts or fresh scat, he yelled, "All clear, James. Bring 'em up."

The cave was just large enough to bring the animals inside. Charlie hung both spare blankets over the opening to help keep the wind and snow at bay and positioned the horses' rumps toward the entrance to further reduce the draft. The animals chomped on their grain. With no room to build a fire, Charlie and James ate cold leftover biscuits and pemmican.

Huddled in their bedrolls with the storm swirling around them outside, they finally relaxed enough to talk about their situation. James didn't know if they were in deep trouble or not, so he asked, "So what do you think, Pa? Are we going to be okay in here? How long do you think we'll have to stay shut in?" He had lots of questions and hoped his pa had lots of answers.

"It's just a spring storm, son. Be over tomorrow, probably, and we'll head home the way we came up so's not to run into trail problems. We'll finish the job down the other side of the mountain to our campsite in Hardpan Basin another weekend, in better weather.

"Now get some sleep and don't be frettin'

yourself none. We'll be okay."

That's all James needed to hear; he trusted his pa implicitly. "'Night, Pa," he said, just before falling asleep.

"'Night, son."

During the last 24 hours, Charlie had began realizing that, along with the pride and comfort a child could bring to a parent, came a huge responsibility for their well-being. *Could be mighty worrisome this business of child raisin'*, he mused as he also fell asleep.

Pulling aside the blankets from the cave entrance the next morning brought Charlie and James face-to-face with a dazzling white wonderland. Sunbeams sparkled off all surfaces: trees, bushes, ledges and rocks. Dawn had brought a new perspective to their world from the previous day's climb. . . and a new set of problems—how to safely descend Table Mountain through knee-deep snow.

Charlie figured the fluffy snow depth would be no problem for he and Rooster to break trail, followed by Dan and then Chester and James. The problem would be potential slipping and sliding down the steep switchbacks—they'd just have to take their chances riding, as walking in the deep snow and leading the animals was a more dangerous option. Charlie wished his horses had caulked shoes on to help grip the snow, but then, he hadn't expected to have to contend with a snowstorm.

Problems began as expected about a half mile into the descent. Chester started sliding on all four feet, with his butt almost dragging in the snow. He'd bump into Dan, and when threatened with being kicked by the mule, his forward motion would switch to reverse and he'd come to a sudden halt. He seemed to be playing and having fun, too young to understand the danger.

Then the inevitable happened at the first steep switchback: Chester slid down to the corner and kept going instead of making the turn. He struggled to get back onto the trail—but too late—the snow was too deep and slippery. Charlie knew what was about to happen and called to James, "Jump off, quick. Let go your horse."

James had the presence of mind to jump to the high side just as Chester rolled down the mountain to his left. The horse did two complete rolls, slid on his side and then landed on the trail some distance in front of Charlie where he got to his feet and shook off the snow.

While James found his way down the snowy trail to catch up, Charlie checked the young horse for bruises and found him sound, although nervous.

Deciding to protect his son against any more mishaps, Charlie told him, "I think I'll ride thisun for a while. Maybe my weight will help him keep his footin', and breakin' trail might make him pay attention more and keep him from slippin' so much. James, you ride Rooster. Dan will follow along by hisself."

The same as with most young horses, Chester liked following and found leading scary. He spooked and tried to turn and run when he suddenly noticed two elk nibbling on sprouting fir buds a mere 50 feet from the trail. They were late migrating to higher grazing grounds. And, he tried to jump Green Creek instead of calmly walking across. He landed in the center, slipped, regained his footing and scrambled up the bank on the other side, snorting his displeasure.

Charlie chucked as he patted the horse and said, "Easy there, boy. You're okay. You'll make a right good lead horse in 'nother year or so.

"James, wanna swap horses again? This here youngun is ready to follow quietly and stop his silliness; besides, the goin's easier from here on down to the ranch."

He handed James the reins and said, "Your horse's done well for a youngster. You can be proud of him, as I'm proud of you, son."

James was pleased with his pa's compliment

and to be astride his own horse again. The snow barely covered the ground once they were off the mountain; the trail dry by the time they reached Wapiti.

By mid-afternoon, they jogged into their ranch to welcomed hugs and kisses from Bertha and Jane.

While Jane was hugging her brother, she whispered, "I'm glad you're back, James. I missed you awfully. . . I think puppies did too," she added.

"I liked traveling with Pa, but I like coming home to you and Ma too." He ruffled her hair with brotherly affection.

As Bertha helped Charlie take off Dan's pack gear, she said, "Have I got a story for you, ol' man!"

"And I have quite a tale to tell you, too, dear!"

* * *

That evening, after little ears that need not hear "parent talk" were sound asleep, they swapped adventure stories. Afterwards, Charlie came to a conclusion: "Bertha, bein' responsible for these younguns is gonna make me an ol' man afore my time."

She considered adding, *and me an ol' lady.*

However, she said reassuringly, "Nah, you're doing just fine, sweetheart; they'll keep us young."

"Yes, dear," was all Charlie said.

THE RACE

Returning from a training ride up Shoshone Canyon, James Daye wiped down his young sorrel stallion, Bridger. They'd made the 20-mile loop in record time today—a little over two hours. He was proud of his colt.

Bridger was an offspring of James's mother's famous mustang stud, Washakie, out of his old mare, Brit. Unfortunately the aging mare died a week after foaling due to a uterine infection. James had slept in the colt's stall, feeding it cow's milk every three hours, for the first two months, before it could eat enough grain and hay to subsist. Since the colt accepted James as his surrogate mother, their bond was exceptionally strong. Coming from mustang heritage, Bridger was sturdy, tough and intelligent. This spring, James was training him for the upcoming Fourth of July Stampede Race in Cody, Wyoming, unbeknownst to his mother. Bertha had won the race on Washakie for the past five years; he figured it was his turn to give it shot. At age 16 and Bertha's right-hand assistant horse trainer, everyone considered him a chip off the old block. Fair-haired and horse-savvy like Bertha, everyone had long forgotten that he was adopted.

"Good boy," he cooed as he rubbed the stallion with an old feed sack and brushed his coat until it was no longer sticky with sweat. "Whaddaya, think, Bridger? Are we ready for the big race?"

The horse nickered and nuzzled James's chest.

"I'll have to approach Ma and Pa real careful-like; they think I'm still a little boy sometimes."

Charlie Daye sauntered into the corral carrying a fork full of hay. "Rode him pretty hard, didn't you James? Any special reason?" Charlie appeared the quiet type but not much got past him.

"Well, actually, Pa, I been wanting to talk to you and Ma about riding Bridger in Cody's Fourth of July Race this year. He's in real fit condition, loves to run and will do anything I ask him. Do you think it would be okay? Do you think we could win?"

"Now just hold on, James, those are two separate questions, and I think we'd better get your ma in on this conversation before we both get into deep trouble." Charlie, a mild-mannered, self-proclaimed mule and mountain man, knew it was in his best interest to always include his ever-feisty wife in family decisions that involved horses.

James finished cooling out his colt, gave him water and left him in the corral. Bridger had priorities of his own as he circled a dusty spot and then lay down and rolled over, twice, twisting and scratching his body each time. When he got up, he shook himself to get rid of excess dirt and then trotted over to the hay to eat.

The undisputed head homemaker in the family was Jane, now 11 years old, going on 20. She had been eager to replace the pain of her dysfunctional childhood with the security of the Dayes' family and home and grew to willingly take over many of the household chores, which pleased Bertha as it left her more time to train horses. Curtains now hung over the windows in the cabin's three rooms, braided rugs on the floor and quilted spreads on the beds, thanks to her ability to sew, braid and quilt—none of which came from Bertha's innate skills. Although Jane rode horses by necessity—when she was asked to accompany the family—she preferred domestic life. She also excelled in school, becoming a teacher's assistant for the younger grades and aiming to be an educator when she grew up. She did, however, absorb Bertha's propensity toward being bossy.

"Now mind you wipe your boots before you step foot in here; I just swept the floor," she demanded as Charlie and James entered the cabin seeking Bertha. "If you're looking for Ma, she's out back plucking a chicken for supper and should be straight in.

"Would you both like some coffee?" she added with less severity. She was never one to withhold kindness; she just liked to demonstrate her power within the family hierarchy, and the cabin was her domain.

Charlie and James knew the game and smiled at one another while accepting the steaming hot coffee.

Bertha, blond hair tousled, dressed in men's trousers overlaid by an apron covered with chicken blood, entered through the rear door. "Howdy, dears, and to what do we owe this manly visit to our kitchen in mid-afternoon? Ain't time for supper yet, and we didn't call for your help," she said sarcastically, wishing she were in the barn, out riding Washakie, or anyplace besides plucking and cooking chicken.

"We have somethin' to discuss with you,"

Charlie said. "Why don't you grab a cup of coffee and join us on the porch?"

"Janie, honey, can you get this chicken stewing while I join the men for a coupla minutes?

"Okay, spit it out. What's up with you two?" Bertha, not one to mince words, blurted out as she flopped into a porch chair. Blue sky and puffy clouds overhead made her want to be riding her horse on this mid-May afternoon . . . maybe tomorrow she'd take a ride up Canyon Creek with Washakie and soothe her irritated mood. A brood mare had given birth to a stillborn yesterday, and a yearling stud colt had come into the corrals that morning with a blown knee—probably got kicked while frolicking around in the pasture. They would both heal, but she always worried about her horse family.

Between her and Charlie, they had two studs, five mares, four geldings, three yearlings, three new foals and two mules. Their goal was to train and sell their young horses between the ages of one and four. They had done well, selling twenty-two head over the past five years. Plus for a $50 stud fee, Washakie serviced ten to fifteen other ranchers' mares each year. . . he was earning his keep.

To Charlie, even after twenty years of marriage and with her sour expression, disheveled hair and blood-splattered clothes, Bertha was still beautiful. He smiled at her warmly and thought, *I am a lucky man.* What he said was, "James needs your advice, dear."

"Ma, you know what a great horse Bridger is; we've raised him ourselves. He's the best colt Washakie has sired, and I know you have plans to use him as stud beginning next year. He's strong, willing, smart and *very fast*—you said so yourself."

"James, get on with it. Nightfall will be here before you get to making your point."

"Well, I'd like to enter him in this year's Stampede Race in Cody. Whaddya think, Ma? Can I?"

There, he'd said it! Sweat began trickling from his forehead down his neck. He was nervous. His ma was not the easiest person to convince of new ideas when it came to horses. He hoped she'd come around.

Bertha was quiet.

James made eye contact with his pa and raised his eyebrows in question. Charlie shook his head slightly indicating to be still.

"James, you're one of the best riders I know, but you are still a boy, and these are *men* you'd be racing against."

"But *you* raced against them, Ma, and you're a woman."

Wrong thing to say, and he knew it the second the words escaped his mouth—too late.

Bertha's face reddened, but she held her temper in check as she tried to demonstrate patience when dealing with family or horses.

"I'll let that pass. However, you know that your pa got attacked and beat up before the first race, and riders tried to knock me off Washakie 'til he outran them. When there's money involved, men get mean and nasty, and I don't want you hurt. And the overland race is twelve miles this year not ten, as the race committee thought it would add excitement to start and end at the stockyards. That means racing through town twice which adds more danger with all them people crowded 'round watching.

"The committee's changed the rules now that Washakie has won the race so many times. The prize money is now split—the winner no longer takes all. First place gets *half* the purse, second gets half the remaining, with third and fourth dividing the rest. Spreading the prize money around is expected to bring many more competitors. And by the way, how would you pay the $50 entry fee?"

James answered eagerly, "I've got $10 saved from my winnings at the Shoshone Shooting Match last fall, and I talked with Mr. Charmers at the Cody stocky pens and he's agreed to pay me a dollar a day to work for him every afternoon through Stampede Week. I'll be cleaning pens, hauling water and feeding animals. And I'll pay you and Pa back if you'll loan me the rest of the money to enter.

"I can still work here mornings and evenings, and I'll exercise Bridger every day by riding him to and from work. I've been training him some this spring, and he's in fit condition already—he's mustang."

"Might be good advertisin' for our ranch and Washakie's ability to sire winnin' offspring, if'n he made a decent showin," Charlie added with a wink to James.

"Let me chew on it awhile," Bertha said, although in her mind she thought: *youth, such enthusiasm, how can I say no.*

"Maybe we can take our two horses for a workout ride in the next few days and see how it goes. Lord knows I need a break from ranch worries," she added.

* * *

Two days later found Bertha and James fording the Shoshone. They planned to ride up the North Fork as far as Grizzly Creek where they would once again cross the river and return via the Canyon Trail.

Stretching east and west, Wapiti Valley ran relatively flat and arid for eight miles, sheltered by the Absaroka Mountains to the north and Wapiti Ridge to the south. Clear-running creeks (runoffs from mountain snow) like Jim, Dunn, Whit and Green irrigated the valley and fed the Shoshone year-round. The Daye family lived about mid-way the valley.

"Let's start out with a controlled hand-gallop. Control is the word to remember. Do not let him have his head early; you need to learn to pace your horse."

After a few miles, Bertha yelled to James, "Let's slow a bit, and, while we still have open ground, we can practice bumping into each other. . . good training for your colt, learning to accept and give body contact."

Bridger's ears flattened the first time Washakie bumped into him, but he didn't stumble or break stride from his canter. He was hesitant to reciprocate and bump into Washakie as horse hierarchy dictates that younger horses respect and give way to their herd elders. However, after a second urging from James, Bridger made brief contact and became more aggressive on the next few bumps.

"Good job," Bertha said, reining her horse down to a trot to give him a breather. "Now let's pick up speed again and practice passing.

Remember, control. Your horse should be willing to pass on command or hold back if you don't feel it's time. I'm going to pull to the front first; you hold back."

This accomplished, Bertha then held Washakie back while James urged his horse to pass. Next, she pulled along side and grinning, she yelled, "Race you to Grizzly Creek."

They were in race mode now, no holding back, no bumping, no passing. Competition was the name of the game as they covered the next mile neck and neck: horses' nostrils flaring, heads forward, manes and tails flying, hooves thundering. Bertha mused, *What magnificent animals.* When she sat upright in the saddle, signaling Washakie to slow down, of course Bridger pulled past them, James grinning, thinking his horse was faster.

She thought, but did not say, *Not yet you don't have the fastest horse, son. Not yet.*

They reined up exhilarated and laughing.

"So how did we do, Ma? Can we race? Can we win?"

"You and Bridger did real good, James. You both need more experience, but you've got six more weeks to practice what we did today.

"Winning! I don't now 'bout that. . . depends on the competition. But you might be able to recoup your money, at least, by coming in among the first four. Let me talk it over with your pa and see what he says about helping with the entry fee."

They rode back to the ranch in relative silence, each reflecting on their horse, racing and future ramifications.

"How'd James and his colt do trainin' with you today?" Charlie asked that evening as they snuggled down into bed. This was their special alone time when they discussed family matters not meant for children's ears.

"They're both willing learners. Bridger is Washakie's best progeny, so far. He's fast as well as intelligent. And you know James is a real good rider, the best for his age."

"You mean like his ma," Charlie injected.

"Yes," she accepted his compliment, "except he's young, as is the colt, and they're both inexperienced when it comes to competing against older men and horses."

"Don't forget his years on the streets of New York taught him survival savvy. Warn him to run his own race and stay away from other riders. . . that's 'bout all we can do, if'n we let him enter, that is.

"You haven't said if *you're* gonna race again this year," he added.

"I like the purse money; it sure helps pay the feed bills. I been thinking I'd race and maybe hold back some to see how James is doin' without actually doggin' him like a protective ma. If'n it looks like he can outrun the others, I'll not pass him. But if he can't, I intend to cross the finish line among the first four to pick up as much money as I can."

"Sounds like you've got a good plan, dear, so let's allow 'em both to get some experience, under your watch, so's they can't fall into too much trouble."

"We'll tell him tomorrow, and I'll work with them when I have time. It's good for me and Washakie to get out and run once in a while too.

"I love you, ol' man," she said, giving him a kiss goodnight.

"I love you too, dear."

* * *

Janie was thrilled to be in charge of the ranch house, and Larry had said he'd see to the animals, so Charlie, Bertha and James planned to stay in Cody over the Fourth of July's two-day celebration. They'd bed down near the cattle pens where the horses were stalled.

Being the Stampede Race winner for the

past five years, Bertha and Washakie led the parade down Main Street, kicking off the first day's activities. Other race entrants pranced and danced behind them.

"Look at that black leading the race bunch; I'd sure like to own him," Brady said, as he spat at the feet of his partner in crime while standing on the steps of the Silver Dollar Bar. He and Hank, regular customers of the bar, had been drinking all morning while the townsfolk began gathering along the street.

"Yeah, and look who's riding him, that Queen of B——s Daye woman, and she's not one to mess with. She'd chew you up and spit you out, so's I heard tell," Hank said.

"She don't scare me none. I like that red one the boy is riding too. He's sure a fiery looker. May be we visit the stock pens later, huh, and see 'bout putting a rope around one, or both, of them cayuses."

James finished feeding up for the evening and headed back to the other end of the pens to sleep by his horse. Suddenly, he heard Bridger's whinny, hooves pounding wood, and Washakie's answering scream. Other horses began stomping and whinnying at the commotion. With pitchfork extended, he bolted toward the noise and his horse.

"Quit trying to rope that black—he looks like a killer anyway—and help me with this red one," Hank said as he threw his lariat over Bridger's neck. Bridger reared and cowered in the far corner. "Throw another over loop over this 'un and let's vamoose 'fore someone hears all the ruckus."

Sneaking into the pens after dark, Brady and Hank had found the black and red sorrel stabled side by side. Not knowing that the red was Washakie's son and it's a stallion's nature to protect his family, they didn't expect such a fuss from him. He lunged at the cowboys with his ears laid flat and his mouth open. When he couldn't reach them to bite, he pawed the front boards of his stall and kicked the sides with his hind feet.

Just as they were unlatching Bridger's stall gate, James rushed into view. "Let him go; he's mine," he demanded.

"Sure kid," Brady answered as he continued to open the gate.

Angered and desperate, James threw the pitchfork. One prong struck Brady's thigh making him release his rope as he howled in pain, "Owww! You little sonofagun; you're as crazy as these horses."

Hank pulled his gun.

"Put that thing away and help me. He's unarmed 'less he comes after us with a muck rake. Let's get outta here.

"You'll pay for this, kid. I promise you," Brady shouted as Hank dragged him out into the darkness.

With James camped outside their stalls—pitchfork in hand—the horses soon settled down. Bertha and Charlie arrived bringing him supper, aghast to learn that there had already been trouble and they hadn't been there to help.

"*I* handled it," James said firmly, not feeling as confident as his words sounded.

"Just the same, you get some sleep, and we'll take turns at watch. No telling who will be around during the night or pre-dawn," Bertha said, worry on her mind.

* * *

The starter's gun began the race at nine o'clock, right on time. Crowds lined the street, thrilled to watch the thirty contenders race through town. There were more racers this year than usual because their chances of winning at least some of the prize money were better. Anxious to race, James sprinted ahead with the lead group. Bertha, more patient, was content to run with the pack.

Charlie watched the crowd, looking for the two cowboys who'd tried to steal his horses. He had not found them around the stabling area or cattle pens nor spotted them on the streets. He didn't know whether to be relieved or worried.

Once out of town, James pulled ahead of the others at an easy gallop. Full of youth and confidence, as well as ignoring his ma's advice, he figured, *I've been training my colt over 20-mile rough courses—12 should be easy.*

Bertha saw him race ahead and thought, *Oh Lord, he's not pacing his horse like we trained, but at least he's running alone and will maybe stay out of trouble that way.*

After pouring whiskey over his wound and wrapping it, Brady and Hank had spent the night plotting their vengeful horse-stealing scheme. They planned to catch their quarry while he was racing. It was just a matter of isolating him from the rest.

James made the task easy.

As Hank stood lookout atop a knoll amongst an outcropping of boulders, Brady, leg wrapped and throbbing, stayed with the horses. "Here he comes, and I can't believe our luck—he's running alone, way out in front," Hank declared, as he descended in a hurry, losing his footing on the loose dirt and cussing as he tumbled to the bottom.

"Shut up and be quiet now. We'll have to seize him quick and haul him off the trail 'fore the others come along. You grab his horse and I'll take care of the kid," Brady ordered.

James, riding confident and quite pleased with himself, too late noticed his horse's head rise and ears prick forward as they entered a draw sheltered on each side by large boulders. Faster than he could react, Brady roped James's shoulders and Hank grabbed his horse's reins. They sped off the race course and over the gully to hide among the cottonwoods.

Bertha became concerned; she could no longer see James. Anxious, she began pushing the black forward, hoping to catch sight of him. Working her way close to the front and still not seeing him, she reined Washakie to a halt. Now convinced that her son was no longer in the race, she began retracing the course and noticed hoof tracks milling around the sand off the side of a draw a half mile back.

She followed the tracks and shortly came upon James. With a mother's concern, Bertha noticed that not only was he tied to a tree, his head was bleeding. "Are you okay, James?" she asked as she leaped from the saddle to free her son.

"Yes, I'm all right, but we have to get Bridger back, Ma." James said as Bertha loosened the ropes binding him to the cottonwood. "They's the same guys as tried to steal him last night, and they can't have gone far. . . he's putting up too much fuss."

"Swing up behind me and we'll find them."

Before long they heard Bridger whinnying and the men cursing and yelling at him as he reared and pulled back, fighting against their ropes.

Bertha gave chase, roping Hank and dragging him off his saddle as she drew her S&W .32 and shot Brady in the shoulder. Already in pain from his leg wound, he toppled off his horse with a scream.

"James, catch Bridger and check him over. If he's okay to continue racing, it's not too late to backtrack to the draw and follow it north toward the river; there you'll meet up with the other racers."

"What about you, Ma? This is *your* race; I can't just leave you here."

"I'll be along soon; don't worry about me—now *go*; and good luck, son."

With unfounded trepidation about leaving his mother with the two outlaws, James did as he was told.

Bertha, mad as a she-bear, trussed the men

up to separate trees, showing no mercy and never checking their wounds. Horse thieves were often hung on the spot. *They'll either live or die,* she thought insensitively as she swung her leg over Washakie with every intention of getting back into the race herself.

"Okay, big fella; it's time to show these guys who's still top-racer around here," she said to her horse as she leaned over his neck, guiding him with her weight and knees over terrain hardly fit for a mountain goat.

Within two miles of Cody, she spotted the stragglers and passed them with the ease of a peregrine overtaking meadowlarks. *Go, Washakie, go,* she whispered into his ears, and he willingly gave it his all, leaving behind seventeen, eighteen. . . twenty-three, twenty-four other racing horses. She had four more to pass as they raced the last mile through Cody. She could now see James up ahead vying for second. She would not go by him, but if she could overtake a couple more riders, she could come in second or third.

And she did.

Charlie was the first to greet them.

"Did you see that?" James said excitedly. "If'n we'd had another quarter mile, Bridger and I'd have won; I know we would have. We'll win next year, for sure."

"Good race, son," Charlie said with pride. "Congratulations."

Bertha smiled and added, "I'm real proud of you and Bridger," realizing because of his youth and exuberance, he hadn't acknowledged that she'd crossed the finish line right behind him, and he'd forgotten she'd stayed behind with the horse thieves longer than he had.

Dismounting, she gave Washakie a hug and said with a hint of sadness, "I think this is the last year of racing for us, big fella. We're both getting too old for all this excitement; let the youngsters have their glory. . . it's their time."

Charlie knew his wife needed her space right now—he said nothing.

She patted her horse affectionately, and he nuzzled her in return. Then she walked with Charlie to collect her hard-earned purse money and send the sheriff after the two outlaws.

EPILOGUE

While guiding guests on a horse pack trip into Hardpan Basin in the Shoshone National Forest, Wyoming, Charlie Daye was mauled by a rogue grizzly. By the time he reached a doctor in Cody, blood poisoning and infection had set in and he died three days later. Bertha buried him in the western corner of their ranch near Green Creek, overlooking Wapiti Valley, a place he so dearly loved. His epitaph read:

Charles Payton Daye 1862 to 1914
A true mountain and mule man.
Loved by his wife Bertha and
their two children James and Jane

In 1911, James married Suzanne McLowry, and together they had three children: Charles, Thomas and Elizabeth. For a wedding present,

Bertha and Charlie gave him 100 acres along Whit Creek, neighboring their land, on which he outfitted guest hunting and pack trips into wilderness areas until he later became manager of Washakie Guest Ranch.

Jane became a schoolteacher at the Wapiti Valley School at age 16. She continued her education at the University of Wyoming and became the principal of Park County schools. She established a children's home in Cody, taking in orphans and waifs, and then she moved to Cheyenne where she helped found the Wyoming Children's Home Society, which functioned as an orphanage and unwed mothers' home. She never married.

Bertha continued raising and training horses on a small-time basis after her husband died. As she reached her middle years, she asked James and his family to combine both ranches into one large guest ranch where she worked and helped manage until she died at age 76. She was buried beside her husband near Green Creek.

Author's Comments

The places and timing of the historic events in these stories I have tried to keep accurate. However, I took a writer's creative liberty to portray characters in a fictitious manner, and their adventures, although in keeping with the times, are a product of my imagination.

More interesting information can be gleaned about the Johnson County War (Wyoming's Civil War), Cody, the Shoshone Dam Project, Annie Oakley, and William F. Cody on the Internet's Wikipedia.com and on WyomingTalesandTrails.com.

In 1895, the Tillett family established the TX Cattle Ranch and still owns a working guest ranch north of Lovell, Wyoming. They played an invaluable role in saving wild horses, especially the Pryor Mountain mustangs.

The Orphan Trains transported over 200,000 children from the East to find homes for them throughout the Mid-West and West from 1854 to 1929—thanks mostly to The Children's Aid Society and The New York Foundling Hospital. Both organizations are still active today in helping children. The pen and ink drawing appearing on page 96 was found on www.nebraskahistory.org.

I used Dave Bragonier's map, which he drew for his Wyoming true adventure book, *Wild Journey,* as a foundation for the maps that appear just before my first story. With his permission I deleted, added, and changed it to compliment my own stories. Thanks, Dave.

Also, my thanks to Karen Lavoie for her proofreading and editing suggestions and to Laura Ashton for her diligence in compiling my manuscript into book form.

You may visit my website:
www.prgottbooks.net
or email me at pgott@gwi.net